MASQUERADE NURSE

MASQUERADE NURSE

JANE CONVERSE

THORNDIKE
CHIVERS

This Large Print edition is published by Thorndike Press®, Waterville, Maine USA and by BBC Audiobooks, Ltd, Bath, England.

Published in 2003 in the U.S. by arrangement with Maureen Moran Agency.

Published in 2003 in the U.K. by arrangement with the author's estate.

U.S. Hardcover 0-7862-5887-X (Paperback)
U.K. Hardcover 0-7540-7726-8 (Chivers Large Print)

The text of this Large Print edition is unabridged. Other aspects of the book may vary from the original edition.

Set in 16 pt. Plantin by Minnie B. Raven.

Printed in the United States on permanent paper.

British Library Cataloguing-in-Publication Data available

Library of Congress Cataloging-in-Publication Data

Converse, Jane.
Masquerade nurse / by Jane Converse.
p. cm.
ISBN 0-7862-5887-X (lg. print : sc : alk. paper)
1. Traffic accident victims — Fiction. 2. False personation — Fiction. 3. Hospital patients — Fiction. 4. Euthanasia — Fiction. 5. Physicians — Fiction. 6. Nurses — Fiction. 7. Large type books. I. Title.
PS3553.O544M37 2003
813′.54—dc22 2003060713

MASQUERADE NURSE

one

Kathy Barrett shifted in her bedside chair, checked her watch, and made a mental note never to envy private duty nurses again.

Several times since Miss Whittaker had come to Knollside Community Hospital, Kathy had hurried past Room 206 to see the 3:00 to 11:00 p.m. special seated in this very chair — a luxury never dreamed of by general floor nurses. On most of those occasions, Miss Whittaker had been engrossed in a paperback novel. At ten o'clock, when your legs ached, and 207 complained of severe intestinal pains, and 204 demanded a bedtime snack that had been expressly forbidden by her doctor, when the Head Nurse was in one of her hypercritical moods, and 212 acted as though you had been personally responsible for his kidney-stone attack, it was natural, Kathy decided now, to indulge in a twinge of jealousy at seeing another nurse *off* her feet. What harried general at Knollside wouldn't envy a special, responsible only to an attending physician who never appeared during the second shift?

But tonight, relieving the special while Miss Whittaker took a ten-minute coffee break in the staff room, Kathy found herself wishing the time would hurry by. In the corridor outside, moving from one lighted summons to another, or exchanging hospital gossip with other R.N.'s at the second-floor nurses' station, the oppressive silence of a single dimly lighted room couldn't creep under your skin.

Miss Whittaker's patient was an old man. Kathy had never been assigned to 207 and her knowledge of the case history was sketchy; at the second-floor desk she had heard that the man had undergone a nephrectomy several months ago. A victim of nephroma, the patient had responded poorly to surgical removal of a kidney wracked by a malignant tumor. Miss Whittaker had mentioned a hepatorenal syndrome — failure of liver and kidney function, a condition usually terminating fatally.

An ominous atmosphere seemed to compress the very air inside the room. A respiratory complication accounted for the only sound; in his drugged sleep, the old man coughed intermittently, a thin, moaning, minor-key hacking not unfamiliar to

Kathy, but as heavy now with preagonal implications as a chilling death rattle.

It could happen any minute, Kathy thought. Now, during the few minutes while Miss Whittaker is having her coffee. The thought struck her as morbid, and perhaps selfish. As though she were hoping the old man would wait until his own nurse was in the room before giving up the ghost! Was anything more callous than wanting a doomed human being to live another five minutes to suit your convenience? Why another five minutes? To awaken from slumber, to face the excruciating pain that scoured his insides when one hypodermic injection wore off and the next took its effect too slowly? The man was only technically alive. He had no hope in life except the promise of painless death. Yet you couldn't help wanting to avoid the depression that inevitably followed you home when a patient expired. No matter how many times you were present at that hairline moment between two inexplicable stages, you never became inured to the shuddering sensation. You always carried it home.

How helpless Miss Whittaker must feel! How the hours must drag in this dreary room! Minor tasks could occupy only moments; keeping this patient comfortable could only mean keeping him asleep. With Dilaudid, probably. Maybe dionin; besides relieving pain, didn't it also relieve the tendency to cough? And decubitus ulcers would have to be avoided; an old, bedridden patient would be susceptible to bedsores. But after the bed was immaculate and the drugs had induced sleep, what then? Wait. Sit here and wait. I'd rather run from room to room, Kathy decided. In most of the rooms, a going-home suitcase sat in the closet, waiting to be packed. In some of the rooms, convalescing patients returned your smile.

Kathy glanced at her watch once more, determined to channel her thoughts into more cheerful directions. But the weak, prophetic cough assailed her ears once more, and when she tried to concentrate on her life instead of on the old man's death, the thoughts were somehow related. Her own father must be this man's age. If he were still alive, and wherever he might be. A few times, between her departure from the orphanage down in Southern California and her graduation from nursing school, she had made a few feeble efforts to find him. Feeble, because she had stopped to wonder why a daughter would want to find a man who had deserted a wife with an eighteen-month-old baby girl in her arms.

There had been vague remembrances of a bitter, poverty-plagued, overworked woman. And a morning when the bitter woman was no longer there to tell Kathy that her father had been "the scum of the earth." Five-year-old remembrances, obscure and almost forgotten now, buried under years of living in a drab, if humane, institution. Seven-year-old chatter late at night in a drafty dormitory. Hearing herself saying, "I do *too* have a daddy! He's looking for me all the time. When I grow up, I'm going to find *him*. You'll see!" And the derisive giggle of other little girls in the darkness; the cottage mother opening the door to shush them with the customary, "That will *do*, girls!"

All of it remembered when Kathy had placed the classified ad to which there was no response and had phoned a few Barretts listed in the San Francisco phone directory. No reason to look for him there; for all she knew her father had gone to Timbuktu. But one night, during her term as a probie, a yearning loneliness had overtaken her and she had made the calls. My God, not even certain that his name had really been Frank Barrett, she had kept that childish promise made in a bleak orphanage, not truly wanting to find what was left of her "family" at all! Yet always wishing there was someone. The way Lynne Haley wished; Lynne, who had "graduated" from the same orphanage, had worked her way through teachers college while Kathy studied nursing, and had miraculously gotten a job upstate at the same time Kathy decided to rent her own apartment and scout around for someone who would share the expenses.

In the past two years, Lynne had become a sister. Not merely because of their amazing physical resemblance: the same unruly, pale honey-colored hair and almost identically shaded deep, slate-blue eyes. These were only superficial similarities. Having shared the same background, the closeness had been almost inevitable. It was a closeness that precluded jealousy when Kathy had introduced Lynne to Jim Stratton after a date, and the young M.D. had promptly fallen in love with the pert kindergarten teacher. Lynne doesn't *have* a family to look for, Kathy thought, but she's going to have one now: Dr. Stratton's people . . . children of her own. Lynne's forthcoming marriage to Dr. Stratton invoked only a sympathetic envy in Kathy and a melancholy realization that in a few weeks she would have to search for someone else to share her apartment in the bustling town near San Francisco.

Miss Whittaker opened the door, breaking the strangely related chain of thoughts. A large-boned, stony-faced behemoth of a woman, she had a voice to match. As she crept into the room, her hushed, professional whisper resembled a whoosh of air rushing through a wind tunnel. "I wasn't too long, was I?"

Kathy rose. "Not at all."

Miss Whittaker edged toward the bed. "No changes?"

"Nothing."

"Well, thanks, hon. I needed a break."

"I can imagine," Kathy said.

The old man coughed again, and Miss Whittaker shook her head. "I have half a mind to send for his family. His wife stays here all day, ever notice? He has two married sons and a married daughter."

"Oh?"

"They come in and out on weekends. Lot of good it does. He has agnosia." Unnecessarily, Miss Whittaker explained, "Can't recognize people, poor guy. But you know, when he's conscious he keeps asking for . . . something that will put him to sleep . . . for good. I've never handled a more hopeless case. He doesn't want to live, but he hangs on . . . day after day."

"It seems almost cruel to keep him alive, doesn't it?" Kathy asked.

Surprisingly, Miss Whittaker's face tightened into a hard, disapproving mask. "I suppose you haven't heard euthanasia is *illegal?*"

Kathy felt herself coloring. "I didn't mean to imply. . . ."

"Well, you watch that kind of talk, hon. I once worked for a doctor who decided to play God. Similar case, too. Terminal . . . cancer. And *he's* not a doctor any more, if you know what I mean. Big, soft-hearted fella. Good doctor, too. They did an autopsy on the patient and fixed the cause of death as an overdose of codeine."

"The patient would have died anyway?"

"In a matter of weeks. *Probably.*" Miss Whittaker raised her thick eyebrows meaningfully. "It's that 'probably' that cost Dr. Schelling his license to practice, and then some." She sighed, shaking her head. "It was a terrible thing. Shocking!"

The coughing sound from the bed was repeated, emerging more like a painful groan this time. She turned away from

Kathy to peer at the old man's face.

"It still seems —" Kathy whispered.

"Cruel," Miss Whittaker mumbled. "I didn't say it wasn't. Just . . . oh, well, when you've been at it as long as I have, you'll know. You don't run around saying it would be more merciful to —"

Kathy interrupted abruptly. "I won't."

"Okay. Thanks again, hon."

"Sure thing."

Kathy slipped out of the room, instinctively drawing a deep breath of regenerative air as she stepped into the corridor.

Miss Whittaker had been right. For every ten terminal cases, somewhere there was a walking miracle whose affliction had once been termed "hopeless." You had to keep remembering the miracles and doing what you could to prolong life, even when your patient begged for release. Still, it was a relief not to be shut into a room where someone's agony might tempt a decision. And it was good to know that there were thick-skinned Miss Whittakers on duty.

Kathy walked toward the nurses' station as though it were an oasis in a parched desert. Midway between 207 and the protruding, semi-circular desk, she became conscious of quick, heavy footsteps behind her. For a moment she thought Miss

Whittaker might have followed her out of the room. Seconds later, it became obvious that the pounding tread was not being made by soft-soled nurses' oxfords. In almost the same instant, Kathy heard her name called by a disturbingly familiar male voice.

"Miss Barrett?"

She wheeled around, verifying that the person who had been hurrying to catch up with her was Ralph Knoll. Yet it was unusual to see the stocky assistant administrator around the hospital after five o'clock. Almost as unusual as the very *existence* of an assistant administrator in a comparatively small, privately owned hospital. Of course there were some who pointed out that Mr. Knoll's job had been created for him because his mother owned majority stock in the hospital and that, in fact, the suburban community had been named for and was largely owned by family, so that the dapper, thirtyish bachelor might as easily have been placed as assistant in any of a dozen Knoll enterprises. But this was staff gossip; Kathy's dislike for the man wasn't founded on the rumor that he neither deserved nor understood his executive position. It was based on the voracious expression in a pair of piggish, watery eyes that appeared surrounded by surplus flabs of paste-white flesh. Seeing that half-derisive, half-approving expression now, it was difficult to maintain an impersonal reserve.

Kathy managed a polite smile. "Yes, Mr. Knoll?"

He was at her side by then, apparently with nothing urgent to say to her. Certainly nothing related to her work. "I didn't . . . see you around the floor. Thought maybe it was your day off."

"Were you looking for me, Mr. Knoll?"

It was an obvious opening, and Kathy regretted the question almost before it was asked.

He must have accepted it as an encouraging remark, because Ralph Knoll appeared more at ease now, a humorless smile stretching his rubbery face. "Why wouldn't I look for you? Girl as pretty as you are . . ."

"I meant . . ."

He was suddenly businesslike and aloof. "No, as a matter of fact, I just happened to be making the rounds."

"I see." Kathy glanced uneasily toward the nurses' station, anxious to end the stilted conversation.

"I'm rarely here at this hour, but it's my

business to check on the staff . . . see that everything's functioning smoothly." Ralph Knoll favored Kathy with a martyred half-smile. "Mine isn't an eight-hour job, you know."

Kathy grinned inwardly at the lame justification. "I'm sure it's not."

"Have you been off the floor?"

The question was ridiculous; if the man had been concerned about an absent member of the staff, he would have consulted the head nurse. Kathy suspected that the uninformed "administrator" would rather be roasted on a spit than ask a question of Mrs. Pick; the 3-to-11 head nurse on this floor had been nicknamed "Ice Pick" for valid reasons.

"I've been relieving Miss Whittaker in 207," Kathy explained.

"Does our staff do this regularly?" Feigning importance, Knoll extracted a leather-bound notebook from an inside pocket of his jacket and proceeded to make a methodical notation of the incident. "Relieve private nurses not on our payroll?"

"The patient pays for full hospital services, Mr. Knoll. And since his family's hired specials, we get more relief than we give. And we wouldn't want Knollside boycotted by specials because we don't allow them time to go the bathroom, would we?"

Ralph Knoll's usually pasty complexion flushed momentarily, and he replaced his notebook and pen. "No, of course not. Unfortunately, I . . . I've been so preoccupied with my desk work . . . supplies, payrolls . . . I . . . haven't had an opportunity to acquaint myself with . . . procedures on the floor."

"I'm sure you'll find Mrs. Pick helpful if there's something you want to know," Kathy said.

"Yes . . . yes, I intend to interview all the personnel, as time permits. I was wondering . . . ?"

"Yes, Mr. Knoll?"

"Possibly you could be helpful. Give me a . . . general rundown on. . . ."

"I'm on duty now. Mrs. Pick is shorthanded tonight and she's waiting for me to —"

"I meant . . . say, *after* you go off duty?"

He had finally gotten to the point, and Kathy felt a wave of pity for the man; he obviously sensed that people disliked him and that he couldn't hope to have an invitation accepted unless he dressed it up with some "logical reason."

"I thought we might stop for a snack somewhere and . . . if you don't have other arrangements, that is. . . ."

It was too painful to watch Ralph Knoll's discomfort. And since she had planned to stop for a late meal before going home, Kathy found herself agreeing to let the "assistant administrator" drive her home when her tour of duty ended at eleven.

She regretted the impulsive acceptance during the next hour. A bus ride and sandwich might be dull, but she wouldn't be uncomfortable. She would be forced to explode his excuse — tell him firmly that he would *have* to get his information from her superiors. And what would they talk about then? One of these days, Kathy assured herself grimly, I'll learn to say no.

Yet, taking care of minor duties in the sleeping ward, she suspected that the day when she could shove aside an unwanted invitation was a long way off. When you were lonely yourself, you empathized with dislikable people, sensing that their loneliness was more acute than your own. A few hours of exchanging awkward sentences with Ralph Knoll wouldn't be disastrous, and she would make certain that his interest in her wasn't encouraged. After tonight she would avoid him. It wasn't the end of the world.

two

Kathy's predictions about the informal date were accurate — at least through cocktails and steaks at an all-night restaurant.

During the dinner, Ralph Knoll made an absurd effort to pretend that they were engaging in a professional conference, asking meaningless questions, the answers to which should have been obvious to the most disinterested layman. Apart from the disturbingly hungry, sweeping surveying of his eyes, his manner was rigidly formal, except for the request that Kathy address him by his first name.

Bored and tired, at twelve-thirty she reminded Ralph that while she didn't go on duty until three, *he* had to be at his desk early the next morning.

Possibly because he had insisted upon ordering drinks after dinner, Ralph loosened up enough to admit that the hospital routine wouldn't collapse if he came in an hour later. Kathy suspected that he knew it could function as efficiently if he didn't show up at all, but there was no other alibi for wanting to leave. Taking advantage of the fact, Ralph ordered a second round of drinks, prolonging the agonizing conversation.

It wasn't until he had pulled his sleek, chromium-dripping convertible to the curb in front of Kathy's apartment that the chunky scion of Knollside dropped his inquiring-executive act. And when he shed the pose, he did so without any attempt at subtlety. As though someone had released a coil spring, he reached out for Kathy, leaving not a split second for protest before she was smothered in a pair of rapacious arms — before the moist, cold flesh of his lips pressed themselves against hers.

Surprised by the sudden move, Kathy stiffened, too overcome by shock to resist. Before fear and disgust prompted a fierce struggle to free herself from the unwelcome grasp, Ralph had released her, but only long enough to mumble a few slurred, incoherent phrases, possessing her mouth once more with a passion bordering on the psychotic.

Lights still burned in the first-floor apartment adjoining Kathy's. A scream would have summoned help. But even though the violent attack had terrified her, it seemed unreasonable to shiver like a frightened child after a vicious twist of her body had shaken her free. Worse, she remained too stunned to move out of the car quickly, too confused to calm the breathless animal at her side with a stinging slap. Besides, anger might have infuriated him. Kathy shifted close to the protective door at her right, her mind groping for words.

Ralph was articulate first. Coldly, his voice strained and unsteady, he said, "I suppose you think you're too good for me!"

There was a chilling threat in the accusation. Kathy continued to search for a pacifying phrase, found none, and placed her hand on the cold metal of the door handle.

"I don't suppose you know what I could do to you if I wanted to get nasty."

Awkwardly, Kathy muttered, "I imagine . . . you could."

He was staring straight ahead of him, past the windshield and into the sparsely lighted, windswept street, his face curiously pale and formless. "Sure you don't want to change your mind?"

Revulsion and uneasiness distilled themselves into pure anger, and now she had words for him: *"You're probably the most detestable person I've ever known!"*

Kathy lifted the latch and shoved the

door open, only dimly conscious of the hatred smoldering in the man's eyes.

"You're going to be sorry, Miss Barrett. . . ."

"What are you going to do, have me fired? Nurses are hard to find. Creeps like you are a dime a dozen!"

Kathy slammed the car door. Something like a raging roar of protest followed her, but she didn't hear Ralph Knoll's parting words. She was running for the apartment house door, not entirely certain the encounter hadn't been part of an upsetting dream. Running and shuddering — pierced by a chill that had nothing to do with the raw December wind from the bay — she hated her own weakness more intensely than she hated the man who had taken advantage of it.

Lynne was asleep when Kathy reached the sanctuary of their apartment. With no one to listen while she related the experience, there was nothing to do but lie in bed, reviewing the unpleasant encounter with Ralph Knoll, tracing the hours back to the interminable session in Room 207, then forward again to the unbelievable episode in the car. Buried deep inside her, there were tears. But whether they were tears of rage, humiliation, or frustration,

Kathy couldn't determine; they refused to materialize and bring relief. She drifted off into an uneasy sleep, wondering what a misfit like Ralph Knoll could possibly do to avenge himself when someone (probably only one of many, yet someone new and aggravating) had rejected him.

At seven the next evening, Mrs. Pick, apparently in one of her rare congenial moods, adjusted her steel-rimmed glasses, softened the scowl that usually creased her thin pink-and-white face, and invited Kathy to have dinner with her in the staff room.

During their meal, after her customary remarks about the inefficiencies of the kitchen help and the ridiculously small pats of butter, the gray-haired head nurse looked up from her tray to fix Kathy with an inquiring stare. Her tone was as crisp as her heavily starched, old-fashioned uniform: "Has Mr. Knoll been pumping you about my wards?"

Kathy hesitated. "He asked a few questions, but I told him to see you." Without going into the more uncomfortable details, Kathy told her superior about the senseless interview. "I don't think he was seriously interested, Mrs. Pick."

"Seems to be interested now."

"In *what,* for heaven's sake?"

The head nurse narrowed her eyes, as if to protect Kathy from their blazing light. "In everything that's *my* business, and the Supervisor's. And none of *his!* I don't say an administrator isn't supposed to know what goes on upstairs. Mr. Anderson certainly does. But he doesn't go around asking the staff questions behind my back."

"As I said, Mrs. Pick, I don't think he was really interested." As delicately as possible, Kathy explained that Ralph Knoll had used the questioning as a blind for strictly personal reasons.

"That may be so, Miss Barrett. But he's been buzzing all over the floor since three o'clock, getting in everyone's way and pumping everybody." "Ice Pick" stabbed at a lamb chop with her fork. "Checking up."

"I'm sure you don't have much to worry about. My guess is that he doesn't have anything better to do and he wants people to think he's working."

"Who said I'm *worried?* I'm annoyed, yes. And I'm going to tell Mr. Anderson I'm annoyed, believe you me." Mrs. Pick's eyes found Kathy's, boring into them suspiciously. "I'm not concerned, my dear. I'm curious as to why he's suddenly so interested in *your* record."

"My *record?*"

"Everything gets back to me, you know. And he hasn't been asking my R.N.'s how I run the wards. He's asked at least four of them questions about *you.*"

"What kind of questions, Mrs. Pick?"

The terror of the second floor paused. "I can't repeat anything specific. Can't recall the exact words, that is. But if I were looking for a reason to dismiss someone, I'd keep probing. Sooner or later I'd find out about some . . . infringement or carelessness or mistake that would give me grounds."

"You don't think he's out to get me fired?"

"I'm telling you how I'd go about it if I were a sneaky, spiteful, spoiled brat who doesn't belong in a hospital — and if I had some sort of grudge."

Kathy couldn't resist a smile. "I appreciate being taken into your confidence. Those are strong words for a head nurse to use about . . ."

"About an administrator? You don't think you'd hear me talking this way about Mr. *Anderson?*" Mrs. Pick's worshipful attitude toward that knowledgeable gentleman was known throughout the hospital. “Oh, no! I just don’t like snoopers. And I don’t like anyone thinking for one minute that I’m not aware of what’s going on, in front of my nose *or* in the corridor. I know *everything,* young lady. I’ve been a nurse for thirty-three years. In thirty-three years you learn to keep your eyes and ears open.” Mrs. Pick shoved her dinner plate out of the way irritably and tasted her dessert before she spoke again. “Terrible lemon pudding. Don’t you think it’s *terrible,* Miss Barrett?”

Kathy sampled hers and dutifully agreed that, yes, it was terrible.

“Bitter,” Mrs. Pick said authoritatively. “Someone ought to get Mr. Knoll to investigate the *kitchen.* What was I saying?”

“That in thirty-three years —”

“You learn to be on your toes. Yes, you do. You even know what the R.N.’s call you when you aren’t around.”

Embarrassed, Kathy started to offer a halting apology, but the older woman wasn’t interested.

“ ‘Ice Pick.’ It’s very appropriate. At least they know I’m not a namby-pamby.”

“Yes, ma’am.”

“Well, there you are! I’ve just proven to

you that I know what's going on, haven't I?"

"You have, Mrs. Pick. Now maybe you can tell me if I should start looking for another job."

"Over my dead body, Miss Barrett!"

Kathy attempted a grateful smile, but it was frozen by the icy glare of her dinner companion.

"Good nurses don't grow on trees. Why do you think I want *you* to know about Mr. Knoll? To keep *you* on your toes, young lady."

"Thanks, Mrs. Pick."

Abruptly, the head nurse dropped the subject. "Miss Whittaker's had her dinner, hasn't she?"

"Yes. Remember, you asked me to stay in 207 so that she could get out? It's such a depressing room to have a tray brought in. . . ."

"I remember *perfectly,* my dear. Five o'clock, wasn't it?"

"Yes."

"Just before Mr. Knoll left the building. He joined Miss Whittaker here for coffee."

"He wasn't interviewing a *special?*"

"I haven't had a chance to ask her what *that* was all about." Mrs. Pick frowned into her coffee cup. "But I will. You can count on that. I'll make it my business."

"You're very thorough, Mrs. Pick."

"Did I ever tell you I've been nursing for thirty-three *years?*"

"Really? That long?"

"Thirty-three long years. Coffee's horrible, isn't it, Miss Barrett? Wouldn't you swear it's chicory?"

With the Ice Pick on your side, you didn't have to be concerned about the meddlesome, vengeful son of Knollside's principal stockholder. Under the circumstances, though the coffee was remarkably good for a hospital, Kathy had no recourse but to agree. "*I'd* say it's chicory. Tastes just *like* chicory."

Mrs. Pick drained her cup in three gulps and nodded triumphantly. "Nobody puts anything over on me. I've been around *much* too long, Miss Barrett. Some day when I have more time, remind me to tell you how many years I've been in the nursing profession."

Shortly after nine, Kathy was in the nurses' station helping Mrs. Pick fill out a medication report for Accounting when Miss Whittaker appeared at the desk. The Amazon-sized special looked grim, and her absence from Room 207 gave further indication that tomorrow she would be available for a new case. Even her customarily bellowing voice was subdued as she said, "Mrs. Pick, would you please notify Dr. Schneider . . . and Mr. Bailey's family? He's gone."

Mrs. Pick rose quietly, accompanying Miss Whittaker to the room, then returned moments later to make the necessary phone calls. Kathy said nothing; other nurses who drifted in and out of the station caught the mood and instinctively spoke in whispers.

Before ten o'clock, the reception room saw a steady procession of relatives: tearful young adults and a stoic, glassy-eyed elderly woman who was led, unseeing, to 207 and emerged half an hour later, still dry-eyed. Kathy glanced into the reception room several times during her passage from one end of the corridor to the other. Once she saw the family group in quiet consultation with Dr. Schneider, catching a few words of consolation and a brief half-sentence spoken by the old physician: ". . . grateful for your permission. An autopsy may help us in aiding other patients. . . ."

It was a series of scenes all too familiar to any R.N. who worked in a hospital. At ten minutes before eleven, after the deceased patient's family had gone home, Miss Whittaker, her coat over her arm and three paperbound novels protruding from her oversized handbag, appeared at the desk.

"Going home?" Mrs. Pick asked inanely. It was quite apparent that Miss Whittaker had no reason to remain until eleven.

Miss Whittaker evidently considered the question too foolish to merit an answer. "I'll probably be seeing you soon. Good night, Mrs. Pick."

"Good night, Miss Whittaker."

Perhaps the special was too upset to notice her; Kathy walked to the edge of the counter. "Good night, Miss Whittaker. I'm very sorry."

Was it imagination, or did the big woman turn her eyes away deliberately?

"As they say, I suppose it's for the best," Kathy persisted.

"Yes," Miss Whittaker said tonelessly. "So they *say*." She addressed her remaining comments directly to the head nurse. "Mr. Bailey didn't even wake up at seven. Usually by seven he needed a hypo. Slept . . . absolutely without pain . . . right to the end."

"That must have been a comfort to his family," Mrs. Pick said.

"Yes, it was. Unusual, though, don't you think? I was about to phone Dr. Schneider when . . . I discovered I couldn't get a pulse."

Once again, the head nurse and the special exchanged good-nights. This time there was no doubt that Kathy had been snubbed. And Mrs. Pick, who prided herself on noticing *everything*, didn't let the unexplainable slight escape her. "That was very rude," she said, after Miss Whittaker had pushed her way through the revolving door opposite the station.

"She's probably a little unnerved," Kathy said.

"A little *odd*, if you ask me." The tiny, hypercritical dynamo in white clucked her tongue disparagingly. "I've been a special. I know how it feels to lose a patient you've been caring for over a long period. But I know bad manners when I see them, too. You see, my dear, Miss Whittaker's only been in nursing for fourteen years. She has a great deal to learn!"

It seemed to Kathy that another nineteen years of experience wouldn't have changed Miss Whittaker's attitude. She was plainly annoyed or angry. Short of having been adversely influenced by her conversation with Ralph Knoll, there was no explanation available. And not even that possibility made much sense.

* * *

It was a relief to find Jim Stratton and Lynne waiting in the hospital parking lot as Kathy crossed it, headed for her bus stop.

No matter how tiring, irksome, or depressing the previous eight hours might have been, one glance at that handsome, enthusiastic pair, and life appeared suddenly brighter.

"Taxi, lady?" Big Doctor Jim had wrapped a topcoat around himself as protection against the clammy wind; Lynne waited in his new Buick sedan, a purchase made recently in anticipation of Jim and Lynne's Christmas trip home.

"You're a beautiful sight!" Kathy said. "Hate to break up your Friday night date, but I'm not going to say, 'You *shouldn't* have!' "

"You aren't breaking up our date. We're *adding* you and making it a party." Jim grasped Kathy's elbow and hustled her into the front seat beside Lynne, circling the car while the girls exchanged greetings.

"Hi, wage slave!"

"Hi, Lynne. I was just telling Jim, tonight I wouldn't have made it home alone."

"Bad day?"

"Gruesome."

Jim Stratton joined them, slamming his

door and starting up the motor. "Who's gruesome? My mother thinks I'm adorable."

"Kathy's had a rough eight hours," Lynne explained. "The way I see it, *any* eight hours working in a hospital would be awful."

Jim laughed. "Listen to her! And *that* woman is going to marry an M.D.!" He turned the car out of the parking area into the street.

"I'm not chopping the profession, honey. I'm just admitting I'd make a lousy nurse." Lynne shook her head. "I'm so squeamish, I'm not even going to ask you what happened today, Kathy. I'd rather not know."

"And I'd rather not talk about it," Kathy said. "Let's talk about your day."

"Oh, that'll be fascinating," Lynne said. "Do you want to hear about the rhythm band or sandbox time?"

Jim faked a bored sigh. "Do we get a choice?"

"Well, there's a difference. During rhythms, the kids clobber each other with tambourines. Sandbox, they have access to little shovels."

"Aren't you glad we work in a civilized atmosphere, Kathy?" Jim, not waiting for an answer, took a hand from the wheel and patted Lynne's arm. "I finally broke down and wrote a letter home, telling the folks we're coming to visit. And guess how I described *you,* sweetheart?"

Lynne giggled. "You probably told them I'm an old-maid schoolteacher."

"No, I was very charitable. I said you're a cute blonde chick, but that you wouldn't know the difference between a scalpel and a steak knife." Jim turned to address Kathy. "Speaking of steak knives, we were thinking of taking you to the Golden Steer. At this hour, it's either that or Hank's Drive-in."

"Don't go to a lot of bother," Kathy said.

"*Bother?* Feeding the girl who introduced me to my old-maid schoolteacher?" Jim laughed again. In the dim light from the dashboard, he looked more like a carefree college kid than a responsible and highly respected physician. Looking at his surprisingly rugged features, and buoyed by the infectious laughter, Kathy congratulated herself upon being able to separate envy from jealousy. A man like Dr. Stratton would be easy to love; and it was a blessing that she hadn't learned to love him. Otherwise the present situation would be intolerable. As it was, she could enjoy Jim's company, share Lynne's happiness, and hope that someday. . . .

"What did your mother think about me from *that* left-handed buildup?" Lynne was asking. "Have you heard from home?"

Jim nodded. "She'd be crazy about you if you were Dracula's daughter. My mother likes everybody. Dane and Petey okayed the cute blonde part, but they can't even *visualize* me marrying a gal who isn't an R.N."

"Dane and Petey?" Kathy asked. "Have I heard about them?"

"His brothers," Lynne said. "Pete's only seventeen, isn't that right, Jim?"

"Right. And all steamed up about going into pre-med. That'll make three of us. That was my Dad's dream. Had to give up medical school because he couldn't afford it, eventually settling for operating a drugstore and hiring a pharmacist. I wish he could have lived to see Petey get his M.D."

Lynne sighed. "At least you still have a family."

"*Do* I! Wait'll you meet them, hon." Jim was silent for a moment, checking a street sign and then making a right turn. "Listen to the dinner conversation at our house and you'll *think* you're in a hospital."

"I feel like an outsider already," Lynne said.

"Uh-uh. You'll join forces with my mother. She'd faint if she had to take a sliver out of your finger. Actually — bear me out here, Kathy — medical people don't resent the fainters. Some of my best friends are laymen. So are my patients. So's my best girl. Where I get bugged is when they start interfering with medical matters."

"How could they?" Lynne wanted to know.

"When they sit on a hospital board and hold the purse strings," Jim said. "When you can't convince them that with the five thousand bucks they want to spend on landscaping and on an entryway statue of Ralph Knoll they should buy new equipment for an antiquated lab."

"Who'd be that stupid?" Lynne asked.

"Mrs. Ralph Knoll II. Ralph Knoll III." Jim looked over at Kathy. "Have you ever met our brilliant assistant administrator, nursie?"

"I've met him," Kathy said quietly. "Thank you!"

"You were probably looking into a crack in the woodwork at the time." Jim's vehement disapproval of Ralph Knoll had erased the pleasant expression from his face. "Since Mama put him on the payroll, it's fight, fight, fight all the way whenever we need something vital. I sometimes think he doesn't really care one way or the other whether we buy new X-ray equipment or immortalize his grandfather in marble. He just gets a sadistic pleasure out of swinging his weight around. One of the lab technicians has a theory that Knoll hangs around to hate doctors and chase nurses."

"Relax, darling!" Lynne said. "You get too worked up over that man. You need a vacation."

Jim agreed. "Have you told Kathy we're leaving on the sixteenth?"

"That's next *week!*" Kathy exclaimed. The time when she would be coming home to an empty apartment loomed depressingly close, but her friends were counting the days with joyful anticipation.

"Up the California and Oregon coast," Lynne said ecstatically. "Then we're going to visit Jim's family. . . ."

"Long enough for my mother to invite half the population to our wedding," Jim added. "It'll take her until after Christmas to organize the kind of production that'll satisfy her. That leaves us with a two-week honeymoon. I can't possibly take off any more time. . . ."

"And I've promised the school board I'll stay on until the new semester," Lynne said. "*If* they let me extend Christmas vacation a couple of weeks. What can they say?"

"It sounds wonderful," Kathy told them.

"It won't be, unless you can come up for the wedding," Lynne said. "What'll I do for a bridesmaid if you can't get off?"

"She'll *take* time off," Jim insisted. "Come up by train, Kathy. The worst that can happen is you'll get sacked."

"If it doesn't happen before then," Kathy murmured. She was sorry she had left herself open to inquiry with the remark. And, seconds later, she was grateful for the sight of the Golden Steer's neon sign. By then the conversation had shifted to more immediate matters and there were no questions asked.

three

When the phone rang at noon the next day, Kathy didn't stir from the dinette table. Jim Stratton hadn't made his Saturday-morning call yet; Lynne rose automatically to answer.

Seconds later, she summoned Kathy to the phone. "It's for you. Mr. Somebody's secretary."

Kathy shrugged her shoulders and set down her soup spoon. "You ought to run a message service, Lynne. You're so *specific!*"

"Maybe she said Johnson," Lynne guessed, returning to her lunch.

It was the administrator's secretary calling from Knollside. Mr. Anderson would like to see Miss Barrett. Could she come to the hospital immediately? To Mr. Anderson's office?

"I'm on duty at three. Could I come in just before?" A crisp, efficient voice made it clear that "immediately" didn't mean at two-thirty. It meant *immediately.* Obviously this wasn't a request; it was a summons.

"It'll take me about . . . twenty minutes," Kathy said. She wouldn't take time to finish lunch. What she had had of it seemed to be stuck, suddenly, midway between her throat and stomach.

"Twenty minutes," the impersonal voice repeated. "Thank you, Miss Barrett."

Kathy heard the clicking sound on the other end of the wire. She felt removed from the scene for a moment, returning to hear Lynne calling to her from the dining area: "You're supposed to put the receiver back where you found it when you're finished."

"Oh. Oh, sure." Kathy returned the phone to its cradle.

"And you're supposed to eat clam chowder while it's hot."

"I don't think I . . . want any more."

"Is something wrong?"

"I don't know."

"What do you mean, you don't know? You look pale, Kath. What did she want?"

"I've got to . . . get over to the hospital right away."

"Some sort of emergency?"

"No. That was the executive office. I don't know why, but Mr. Anderson wants to see me right away."

"Well, think positively. Maybe he's going to promote you to —"

"I don't think so, Lynne." Kathy started for her bedroom. "Look, I've got to get dressed."

Lynne was on her feet, an expression of deep concern in her eyes. "Did something happen, Kath? You said you had a bad day yesterday. Did you . . . make some kind of mistake, or. . . ."

"I haven't done anything wrong!"

"Then don't be so edgy! I'm only trying to —"

"I'm sorry, Lynne. And there's nothing to worry about, so forget it, will you?"

Lynne nodded, not wholly convinced. "I just don't understand why you should be shaking like a leaf when there's nothing wrong."

I don't understand it either, Kathy thought. Dressing, riding the bus to Knollside Hospital, walking the endless first-floor corridor to the administrative offices, she asked the question of herself repeatedly. Why should she tremble inside with an instinctive dread when her conscience and record were perfectly clear?

Kathy's intuitive reaction had been justified. She knew it the instant Mr. Anderson's prim secretary ushered her into the huge office, closing the door behind them. Knew it in one breathless scan of faces.

Seated in a stiff semicircle around the administrator's desk were Dr. Ostreicher, senior staff physician, Dr. Newman from Pathology, Dr. Jim Stratton, and Mrs. Pick. At Mr. Anderson's right, Ralph Knoll, impeccably suited, toyed with his little leather-bound notebook. Jim managed a smile of greeting. It seemed that the others present appeared uneasy, as though Kathy's entrance into the room had embarrassed them.

Mr. Anderson, lean, silver-haired, and always mild-mannered, rose from his chair, an unnecessarily gracious gesture, which added to Kathy's discomfort. An exceptionally considerate man, it would be like him to precede an unpleasantness with this extra effort at kindness. Still, his voice retained its usual soft, muted quality. "Ah, Miss Barrett. Good. Now we're all here except Dr. Schneider. You say he's in Surgery, Miss Richards?"

Mr. Anderson's secretary said, "Yes, Mr. Anderson," and took a chair behind her employer's desk. Another folding chair had been provided for Kathy, between Dr. Newman and Mrs. Pick.

"Please sit down, Miss Barrett." Mr. Anderson waited until Kathy had done so before he took his seat again. "I'll get to the point as quickly as possible. First, I want you to know that you're only here because we know you're as interested in the welfare and reputation of Knollside as . . . any of us here. If there was any reason to believe that there had been a . . . breach of . . . ethics, we'd have our interview in private. As it is, an unfortunate circumstance faces us and we're all anxious to . . . reach an explanation, if possible — before the medical examiner arrives. I'm sure we can count on your cooperation."

Kathy's bewilderment must have been apparent to him. Mr. Anderson cleared his throat, studied a typewritten hospital form on his desk for a few seconds, and then said, "Last night one of Dr. Schneider's patients passed away. Not unexpectedly, as you probably know, Miss Barrett."

"Yes, sir."

"Mrs. Bailey gave her consent to an autopsy. I believe you know Dr. Newman — our senior pathologist?"

Kathy nodded dumbly.

"According to Dr. Newman's report, the cause of death was established as an overdose of Nembutal."

Kathy caught her breath. The implications, as far as the hospital was concerned, were devastating enough. But why the deadly silence? Why was everyone deliberately staring into space as though she weren't in the room? Everyone was grave and uncommunicative — except Ralph Knoll. His demeanor approached a look of smug, self-righteous satisfaction.

"I don't know what to say," Kathy half whispered. "I . . . saw the patient . . . several times. But I don't know how I can help. . . ."

Dr. Ostreicher, a portly, balding man in his sixties, interrupted. "You relieved the special duty nurse at five o'clock, Miss Barrett?"

"Yes, Doctor. She left the room for about —"

"Twenty minutes," Mrs. Pick said firmly.

"Was this a usual procedure?" Dr. Ostreicher asked.

"Certainly not, Doctor," Mrs. Pick bristled indignantly. "It happened that Miss Whittaker complained of a headache and asked to be relieved. Normally, her tray was brought into the room."

"During this period, was Miss Barrett instructed to give the patient any medication?" Dr. Ostreicher persisted.

"If she *had*, Doctor, it would be recorded on the patient's chart." Mrs. Pick removed her glasses, breathed on them heavily, and polished the lenses with a handkerchief, as though she hoped the furious effort might dissipate her irritation. "Since it *isn't,* you may safely assume that she didn't."

The elderly physician fell into silence, apparently willing to let someone else expose himself to Mrs. Pick's acid tongue.

Jim Stratton's questioning was more gentle. "Did you notice anything unusual in the patient's condition while you were in the room?"

Kathy thought for a moment. "No. He was asleep . . . I assumed under sedation. Oh, yes . . . I did notice that he didn't cough. The night before, his rest had been troubled by an occasional cough."

Between sentences, the only sound in the crowded office was the scratching of Miss Richards' pencil against her shorthand notebook. Ralph Knoll was recording the comments silently with a ball-point pen.

Absence of the cough was verified by an examination of Mr. Bailey's chart.

"That's all, Miss Barrett?" Mr. Anderson asked. "Take your time. Try to think of any observation that might be helpful to us."

Kathy reviewed the twenty-minute period in her mind. "I can't think of anything else, Mr. Anderson."

Ralph Knoll's voice came through high-pitched and jarringly loud in the solemn atmosphere. "You're aware, Miss Barrett, that from three o'clock until Mr. Bailey succumbed, you and Miss Whittaker were the only people who entered the room?"

"That's ridiculous," Mrs. Pick snapped. "I talked to Miss Whittaker *in the room* at least three times."

"I stand corrected." Ralph's polite sarcasm drew a glare from Kathy's head nurse and a general shuffle of annoyance throughout the room. "But I don't believe *you*, Mrs. Pick, had made any previous comments to the effect that the patient should be put out of his misery!"

Jim Stratton sprang out of his chair. "See here, this isn't a jury trial! It's not a trial *at all*. . . ."

"I think this line of inquiry —" Mr. Anderson began.

"— is exactly the kind the authorities will launch," Ralph cried out.

"We're trying to establish medical facts," Jim shouted. "If you'll stop pretending you're a TV detective and —"

"Gentlemen!" Mr. Anderson's order, spoken more quietly than the heated words fired across his desk, carried with it a ring of authority. Miss Richards' pencil scratched louder and faster. "Gentlemen, please! Under these circumstances —"

"I'm merely pointing up a fact that's entirely relevant," Ralph interrupted, making an effort to control his volume. "Miss Whittaker reported to me a conversation she had with Miss Barrett on Thursday night. I don't think Miss Barrett will mind admitting that she . . . considered it 'cruel to keep him alive'?"

Kathy felt warm blood rushing to her face. With all eyes turned in her direction, she stammered, "I may have . . . said something like that. But it was only —"

"Only your personal inclination regarding —"

Jim had resumed his place, but now he reached forward to pound an angry fist on the desk. "Mr. Anderson, I resent these tactics!"

"I'll leave it to *medical* opinion," Ralph said cuttingly. "If a nurse has expressed herself as favoring euthanasia, and the *next day* a patient succumbs from an overdose —"

"I don't think this is the place for —" Dr. Ostreicher's sentence went unfinished.

Ralph Knoll's voice, rising to a near-hysterical pitch, filled the room. "You doctors and nurses stick together, don't you? Well, I'm interested in protecting this *hospital*, not a nurse who favors putting patients out of the way because —"

"Mr. Knoll!" The chief administrator's shocked tone found an echo among the staff members. "Mr. Knoll, I think this is entirely out of order."

"Is it?" Ralph hurled his question at the senior physician. "Dr. Ostreicher, would you trust a patient with a nurse who favors —"

"I didn't say I favored euthanasia!" Kathy cried. "I only said. . . ." She paused, gasping for breath.

"Miss Whittaker can tell these gentlemen *exactly* what you said," Ralph purred. "She remembers well enough to be convinced that you —"

Jim Stratton was on his feet once more. "Mr. Anderson, if we're going to point a suspicious finger at Miss Barrett on those grounds, then you'll have to include most of the staff! There isn't one nurse. . . ." He stopped to fix Dr. Ostreicher with a meaningful stare. "Not one nurse *or* doctor who's worked with a terminal case involving extreme suffering, who hasn't . . . to whom the thought hasn't occurred. We're human beings! We dismiss the thought, sure. On moral, ethical, religious . . . sometimes only on legal grounds. But if you've practiced long enough, at one time or another you've watched a patient's agony, knowing you couldn't save him, and have asked yourself, 'Why?' This doesn't make us criminals!"

"Dr. Stratton shouldn't accuse me of pretending to be a TV detective," Ralph said unctuously. "He seems to have been influenced by a few medical heroes himself."

Kathy shuddered at the man's easy articulation. In asking for a date, Ralph had been pathetically awkward. Now, driven by an injured ego, the words came to him easily.

"And Dr. Stratton seems to forget, in his flowery speech, that Miss Barrett was with the patient several hours before his death. And that he *did* die of — I believe you medical people call them 'unnatural causes.' "

"I had no reason!" Kathy murmured. "I wasn't emotionally involved with the patient. I felt sorry for him, yes, but —"

"But anyone who knows anything about hospital procedure," Mrs. Pick cut in, "knows that the head nurse dispenses drugs — and only on doctor's orders. The rest of the time they're kept under lock and key. Now, Mr. Knoll, would you like to ask *me* any questions?" Mrs. Pick's voice stabbed through Ralph's vicious accusations, silencing him. He pretended to study the jottings in his notebook, and Kathy noticed that his forehead looked suddenly glazed with perspiration.

Mrs. Pick addressed herself to Mr. Anderson. "Sir, I've been in my profession for *thirty-three years.* That's a long time! But I've never yet seen a conscientious nurse harassed because a special with a good imagination —" she turned a stony glare toward Ralph Knoll "— and someone with a personal ax to grind put their heads together!"

Mr. Anderson, upset by the clash of tempers, must have sensed a new outbreak of hostility. In a pacifying tone, he said, "Now, Mrs. Pick, perhaps Mr. Knoll was a bit overzealous, but we all know he has our best interests in mind. We mustn't assume —"

"I'm not assuming, I *know!*" Mrs. Pick waved a long finger at the lanky man behind the desk. "Personal grudge. You can dismiss me if you like, but I know everything that goes on in my wards. And a few things besides."

Dr. Newton, who hadn't said a word until then, complained that the meeting was completely out of hand and that he had important work to do downstairs.

Mr. Anderson accepted the suggestion with relief. "We'll probably get further with Dr. Schneider present."

"Might be better *not* to have a ready-made explanation for the M.E." Dr. Ostreicher agreed. "He'll cover the same ground, probably arrive at the same conclusion we'd reach here. And we won't have all this . . . bickering."

"Unethical as hell," Dr. Newman grumbled. "When you think of the visitors the man's had . . . and Nembutal available. . . ."

"By prescription," Dr. Ostreicher reminded him pointedly.

"They're hard to come by?" the dour little pathologist asked. He pushed his chair back, and as if by some tacit agreement the others got to their feet with him.

"I expect the medical examiner will be talking to all of us individually." Mr. Anderson stood up, towering over everyone but Jim Stratton. "I hope none of you have planned any weekend trips."

There was a general murmur of disapproval, and then Ralph Knoll, probably desperate to save face and recoup forces for his attack, turned to Mr. Anderson. "I think the authorities will take a dim view of our returning our . . . mercy-loving nurse to the floor. At least, until this matter's been cleared up, I should say."

Mr. Anderson hesitated, his long face creasing in deep lines. "Dr. Ostreicher?"

"I think it might be a wise precaution," the senior physician said sagely. "I think you understand our position, Miss Barrett?"

Kathy swallowed hard. "Yes, Doctor."

"We want the authorities to know we're extremely cautious," Mr. Anderson explained. "A day or two off — you might welcome that. I'm sure this has been a trying experience."

Kathy saved him the embarrassment of additional explanations. "I understand perfectly, Mr. Anderson."

Jim muttered something under his breath and joined the others in a mass exodus from the room. Only the administrator, his secretary, and his assistant remained in the office. Mr. Anderson looked wrung out — with the worst of his ordeal still to come. Miss Richards studied her shorthand notebook, frowning at a notation and correcting it with eraser and pencil. Ralph Knoll feigned interest in the pathologist's report on the desk.

Mrs. Pick and Kathy waited until the

doctors had disappeared from sight at the turn in the corridor before starting toward the elevators.

They walked silently for a minute or two, Mrs. Pick's short, brisk steps rapid enough to keep pace with Kathy's longer stride. There was no one waiting at the elevators; apparently the doctors had headed for a post-mortem in the first-floor coffee shop. Mrs. Pick pushed the "Up" button.

"I guess I . . . won't be going up with you, Mrs. Pick," Kathy said lamely. "I hope you won't be too busy . . . a nurse short."

"I have two hours with nothing to do but find a sub," Mrs. Pick said sharply. "I always have everything under control. See that *you* do, young lady!"

Kathy shifted uneasily. A red arrow indicated that Mrs. Pick's elevator was on its way down. "Oh, I'll be all right. I guess they'll . . . call me if they want me."

"They always do. When you've been at it as long as I have, you'll know that."

"Mrs. Pick. . . ."

"Mm?"

"I don't know how to thank you. If you and Dr. Stratton hadn't been there —"

"Dr. Stratton spoke his mind and I spoke mine. You don't thank people for doing that, Miss Barrett."

"Just the same, it helped to know somebody believed I didn't. . . ." Kathy fought back the tears that were welling in her eyes. "I *couldn't*. . . ."

The automatic elevator thumped to a stop and its doors wheezed open to reveal an empty cage.

"Don't ever say you *'couldn't.'* None of us know what we could or couldn't do. I happen to believe you *didn't*. There's a big difference."

"But you . . . really, you jeopardized your own job telling Mr. Knoll —"

"Didn't jeopardize a thing. He's a fool, mind you. But not fool enough to think this place can get along without me!"

Mrs. Pick moved toward the elevator. Kathy's arm shot out in an unconscious motion, her fingers squeezing the older woman's skinny hand affectionately. "You're a wonderful friend, Mrs. Pick."

"*Ice* Pick! Don't think you'll get on the good side of me with sentimental hogwash, Missy!"

Mrs. Pick marched into the elevator, her thin shoulders rigid. "I'll see you tomorrow Miss Barrett."

"I hope so."

The handkerchief with which she had cleaned her eyeglasses was still in Mrs.

Pick's hand. Kathy watched as she dabbed it at her eyes, then her nose, reaching out immediately afterward to poke a vexed finger at the second-floor button. "Coming down with a cold," Mrs. Pick sniffed. "Bad drafts in this place. Terrible, aren't they?"

"Terrible."

There was one second in which to speculate on how many times in thirty-three years anyone had called the Ice Pick a wonderful friend. Then the doors came together with a soft pneumatic wheeze, leaving Kathy to wonder about an emotional problem of her own.

Where did you go? What did you do all alone between three and eleven when you weren't trusted and couldn't report for duty?

four

Kathy returned to the hospital later that afternoon, in response to a second summons from Mr. Anderson. He phoned personally this time, assuring her that questioning by the authorities would be conducted in private — a veiled assurance that Ralph Knoll would not be present.

Mr. Anderson was right. Kathy's interview, conducted by the taciturn, unsmiling medical examiner, was a quiet, businesslike session, devoid of accusations, implications, or dramatic flourishes. To the straightforward questions, Kathy provided calm, honest answers, including those to which Jim Stratton had objected so strenuously earlier in the day. In all fairness, Kathy concluded, her personal attitudes toward "mercy killing" *did* have a bearing on the case. Discussed in a respectful manner, the subject became less touchy. She felt no resentment, and sensed, when the interrogation was over, that the official had believed she was telling the truth.

But she left the office with nothing more

than a polite thank-you. There was no indication that she had been cleared, no assurance that she would be called back to work the next day.

Nor was there a call from Mr. Anderson's office on Monday or Tuesday. On Wednesday morning, unable to tolerate the suspense, Kathy phoned the supervisor of nurses and learned that she was listed as "suspended." A second call, to Miss Richards, elicited the information that the investigation hadn't been concluded, and that there was nothing Mr. Anderson could do about reinstating Miss Barrett until the case was closed.

Kathy exhausted all the possible time-consuming chores around the apartment before half the week was over. All the books she had looked forward to reading when time permitted held no interest for her now that the hours lay heavy on her hands. And on Thursday afternoon, undistracted by a movie she had been anxious to see, Kathy walked out of the theater during the first twenty minutes of the picture. With no strong personal alliances, apart from Lynne, Kathy's world revolved around her profession. Torn abruptly from work that fulfilled an inner need — the gnawing need to be needed and wanted —

she felt disoriented, an alien on a strange planet where no one required her ministrations, no one looked to her for surcease from pain or for an uplifting smile.

Ironically, she found herself avoiding the few casual friends she had made among the nurses at Knollside. As eager as she was for news from the hospital, Kathy refrained from calling the girls who worked on her shift. When Lynne relayed a message from one of the 3-to-11 R.N.'s, taken during Kathy's absence, Kathy didn't return the call. Arlene would ask questions to which there were no answers; certainly the second floor would be buzzing with gossip, and though the other employees might be sympathetic, a suspension couldn't help but be viewed with raised eyebrows.

Worst of all was the unjustified, engulfing sense of guilt. It was a false sense, of course. Yet when you were suspected, interviewed, distrusted, and cut off from the responsibility and society around which your life revolved, the guilty sensation seeped into your consciousness. Kathy awoke more than once from a stage midway between nightmare and conscious daydream, a clammy chill possessing her body and her pulse racing, remembering a scene in which she pressed a lethal dose of barbiturates into the desperate clutch of an emaciated hand.

"It's frustration," Lynne told her on Thursday evening, when Kathy described the disturbing dream. "You know you're innocent and you can't prove it. Honestly, you'd think they'd have it figured out by now. It's downright vicious to let you torture yourself this way."

They were clearing away the dinner dishes, neither of them mentioning that tomorrow would be Lynne's last day in the apartment. Tomorrow Lynne's Christmas vacation began, and early Saturday morning she and Jim Stratton would be on their way to Oregon.

"Has Jim heard anything?" Kathy asked.

"I've barely seen him, Kath. He's been so busy tying up loose ends so that he can get away from his practice for a month. He'll be here any minute and we're planning to spend the evening at home . . . with you."

"Maybe he's heard something at the hospital," Kathy said hopefully.

She clung to the hope until seven-thirty, when Jim settled himself on the sofa with Lynne at his side, puffing morosely on a half-dead pipe and deploring the injustice of Kathy's situation.

"They can't keep Kathy off her job indefinitely, can they?" Lynne complained. "Suppose they *never* find out who gave that man the . . . whatever it was. It's bad enough to be out of work just before Christmas, but. . . ." She shook her head, letting the sentence go unfinished.

"Apparently nothing's going to change until the authorities can talk to Mrs. Bailey," Jim said.

Kathy frowned. "They haven't talked to her yet? Of course, the family's probably not under suspicion. Miss Whittaker and I were the only. . . ."

"Mrs. Bailey was with her husband during the afternoon visiting hour. Left just before you came on duty." Jim's face registered a sudden alertness. "I haven't seen you since I talked with Dr. Schneider, have I? I meant to keep you posted, but this has been such a hectic week!"

"I haven't heard anything new," Kathy told him.

"Well, it's a rough go. Schneider tells me he prescribed Nembutal for Mrs. Bailey about two months ago. She wasn't able to sleep — apparently Bailey had been through the mill with one complication after another. There's a question about whether or not *he* would have known what the pills were. That's assuming she *didn't* take them herself and later brought them to her husband. He no longer recognized his family, you know."

"I know. But there's a new possibility now? Mrs. Bailey?"

"Can you think of someone with a stronger motive?" Jim's face clouded. "We can assume she loved the man. If *you* were disturbed enough to make an unethical remark, think how *she* must have felt."

They were quiet for a moment, and then Lynne asked why no one had even talked with Mrs. Bailey when Kathy's suspension was still in effect.

"She's in a state of shock, I'm told. Schneider says she hasn't uttered a word since it happened . . . just sits and stares. Evidently no one can get through to her." Jim shot a regretful glance toward Kathy. "Doesn't help your status, does it? And Knoll's being downright vicious about keeping the spotlight on you. I don't get it, Kathy. I've always figured the guy as odd, to say the least. But he seems to be *obsessed* with cutting your throat. Anderson can override Knoll just so far, and then he's got to remember whose family *owns* the hospital. You know the spot he's in."

"Mr. Knoll's got to have *his* way, or he

goes berserk. I found that out." Kathy had told Lynne about the unfortunate "date" with Ralph Knoll earlier. Now she brought Jim Stratton up to date.

When she had finished, Jim relighted his pipe, apparently mulling over her words. He smiled suddenly. "You know something? The Ice Pick had it figured. This afternoon in the coffee shop she bent my ear for over fifteen minutes with her theory on the subject."

Kathy brightened at the mention of the head nurse's name. "Mrs. Pick doesn't have theories, Jim. She doesn't *think* such and such took place. She *knows!*"

"She knew enough to call the shots on R. K. III," Jim agreed.

"Do you want *my* opinion?" Lynne got up, starting for the kitchen. "I think you're dealing with some kind of a nut. And you know something else? No matter how this thing turns out, if this Knoll character's mean enough to practically accuse you of murder just because you didn't let him maul you —"

"I was just thinking the same thing," Jim broke in. He turned to Kathy, his tone grave. "Face it, girl. If you win this round — and I'm sure you will — he'll really have it in for you."

"I'm plugging in the coffee pot," Lynne announced from the kitchen. "Don't say anything crucial till I get back."

"What you're telling me is that I can't ever go back to work at Knollside," Kathy said. It was a relief to verbalize the thought; for nearly a week she had tried to crowd it out of her consciousness. Yet if the fact was obvious to someone as detached from the situation as Lynne, it was time to . . . what had Jim said? "Face it, girl."

"I'm not saying you don't have a choice," Jim explained. "Every doctor I know would turn the place inside out if you weren't reinstated once this mess is cleared up. The point is, you'd be under pressure if you went back. As long as His Highness is around." Jim made a disgusted grimace. "And it looks as though he'll be around for a long time."

Lynne had rejoined them during Jim's evaluation, her expression indicating that she hadn't missed out on any of the conversation. And you always knew when one of Lynne's "tremendous inspirations" had come over her; she stood in the center of the room, impatiently waiting for her turn to speak. Jim stopped to catch his breath, and she plunged in. "Kathy, you're coming with us Saturday!"

"Crazy!" Jim said.

Kathy shook her head. "Crazy-insane."

"No, crazy-wonderful. It's a cool idea."

"And it's *my* idea," Lynne argued, "so I'll do the talking. Lookit, Kath, we want you with us for the wedding, right? So you'd have to come up to meet us anyway. In the meantime, what? Spend Christmas all by yourself in this dumb apartment? Feeling as miserable as you do? Uh-uh!"

"You're both awfully sweet," Kathy said firmly, "but you're out of your minds. First place, you don't invite people to go along on your honeymoon trip. . . ."

Lynne laughed. "It better *not* be a honeymoon trip! Get the chronology straight, dear: A. Trip to Oregon. B. Wedding. C. Honeymoon. *In that order!*"

"She's a stickier for details, this girl," Jim sighed. "Now she's lining up a chaperone!"

"Second place," Kathy argued, "Jim told his family to expect *him* and one strange female, not a harem. I wouldn't dream of barging in. . . ."

"My mother isn't happy unless someone's barging in." Jim was on his feet now, joining Lynne in what struck Kathy as a heartwarming third degree. "The house is enormous, and she's frustrated if there's an empty room in it."

"Gee, wouldn't it be a ball?" Lynne was repeating, partly to herself, partly to Jim and Kathy.

"I *couldn't.*"

Kathy's statement was counteracted by a barrage of sound reasons why she *could* — and should. What was she going to do, wait around to be called back on a job that would be precarious and unpleasant? Spend the holidays alone, when she could be with friends who *wanted* her company?

"If I were you," Lynne said emphatically, "I'd have the pleasure of waiting until I'm called back — and then I'd tell Mr. Knoll *personally* that I wouldn't work in the same building with him. That's what I'd do. That's what *you're* going to do, baby."

"That's telling her!" Jim said. "No back talk. I'll pour the coffee, and let's stop quibbling. It's all decided, Katherina."

Kathy attempted one final, feeble protest. "Your family —"

"My family's going to include my wife's family," Jim said.

Lynne threw her arm over Kathy's shoulder. "Hear that? And up until now, you're all the family I've ever had, Kathy."

"I think . . ." Kathy said weakly, "I think

. . . I'm going to cry."

"Don't waste too much time," Jim yelled from the kitchen. "You'll have to pack, y'know."

"If she wants to cry, that's *her* business," Lynne shouted back. "Shows how much you know about women, Dr. Stratton."

They were working desperately hard not only to convince her that she should come with them but also that they weren't extending the invitation out of pity. And they were succeeding, because there was no doubting their sincerity. Why *not* go? Kathy wondered. When the present was so dismal and the future so uncertain, what was there to be gained by resisting the temptation to escape, if only for a few weeks? With friends like these, refusing out of pride would be tantamount to an insult. Why *not* go? She said it aloud, surprised by the strength in her voice. "Why *not* go?"

Lynne hugged her impulsively. "Now you're making *sense!*"

And minutes later, Jim Stratton raised his coffee cup in a facetious toast. "She who fights and runs away, lives to give Ralph Knoll a piece of her mind another day."

It wasn't easy to laugh when the mention of a name conjured up a rush of depressing images. But in this congenial atmosphere, with the sudden exciting promise of a holiday trip opened up before her, Kathy found it *possible* to laugh. A few hours ago, she would have sworn that there was no laughter left inside her.

five

At the crack of dawn on Saturday morning, Kathy and Lynne were groggily sipping coffee and wondering if Jim had really *meant* five-thirty a.m. when he had *said* five-thirty a.m., when a loud, rhythmic knock on the door sounded through the apartment like an artillery barrage.

Lynne put her cup down. "I guess he wasn't kidding." The loud rapping was repeated as she staggered to the door, her eyes only half-opened. "Ye gods, wake up everybody in the building, why don't you?"

From the moment the door was opened to admit Jim Stratton, it was impossible to be sleepy, quiet, or uncoordinated. His exuberance filled the apartment. "I thought you'd be waiting at the curb! Still having breakfast? Hey, we want to get there by daylight . . . let's go!" Lynne's laughing attempts to silence him went unheeded. "What's with all the shushing? It's *late*."

Somehow, though Jim's infectious enthusiasm had passed itself on to Kathy and Lynne, they got it across to him that not everybody within the radius of a mile was leaving for Bayport, Oregon, this morning. A few of the apartment dwellers might be considerably more interested in sleeping than in the fact that James Stratton, M.D., was embarking upon a venture from which he would return as a married man. Nevertheless, the carrying of luggage and the last-minute admonitions to shut off the gas, close the windows, and lock the doors were managed by Jim with a maximum of thumping, shouting, and door-slamming. By the time the new Buick had roared away from the curb, Kathy was inclined to agree with Lynne: "You know . . . something tells me nobody in the neighborhood is sorry to see us go!"

Kathy settled herself in the back seat of the sedan, still not quite certain that it was really happening. As Jim had pointed out, this wasn't a journey into outer space, nor yet a 'round-the-world cruise. Bayport was less than four hundred and fifty miles up the coast, and they could expect to arrive at the Strattons' by daylight. Still, when the only trip you had ever taken was a bus ride from Los Angeles to San Francisco, the prospect of the carefree ride along a wonderfully scenic coast was exciting. But it was more than that; as Jim's car blended into the sparse early-morning traffic along Highway 101, Kathy realized that what lay ahead became doubly intriguing when nothing but humiliation and unpleasantness lay behind you.

Not that she wasn't anxious to return, to get what satisfaction she could out of being completely vindicated. But Jim and Lynne had been right; she could never go back on duty at Knollside. She would have to become accustomed to change, perhaps to moving to another area. With Lynne married, everything would be different. And this method of stirring yourself out of a rut was the best imaginable; how dismal it would have been if she hadn't let the others talk her into breaking out of that miserable shell!

Along the coast, the air was brisk and cool, blowing away the last traces of morning fog by ten o'clock. Every bend in the highway disclosed new, incomparable vistas: the Pacific an endless, deep calendar blue under the brilliant sun, breakers exploding into a dazzling white spray against the rock-strewn coast or lapping gently against the glassy sand of a storybook bay.

Kathy alternated between enjoying the lighthearted repartee between Jim Stratton and Lynne and feeling a poignant tug of wishfulness. They included her in their circle, yet they were in love, and there were moments in which their rapport served only to accentuate her aloneness. And it seemed that every so often, Lynne, who was capable of remembering the same feeling of not belonging to anyone, would deliberately introduce a subject on which she and Kathy were agreed, so that the two of them would be aligned against Jim. So that I won't feel excluded, Kathy thought — at the same time admiring the sensitivity with which Lynne maneuvered the conversation so that the attempt didn't appear too obvious.

One of the mild altercations involved photography, Lynne begging her fiancé to stop at every turn so that she could record the view on film, and Jim insisting that she wait until they crossed the border. "Wait'll you see *Oregon*," he would insist. "Makes your home state look *dull* by comparison."

And Lynne would argue, "How do you like a guy who spends so much money buying me an expensive camera for an engagement present that he can't afford an engagement ring? And then the payoff: he won't even stop so I can take *pictures* with the thing!"

They made a running gag out of this

issue all the way to Crescent City, where they had lunch on a rocky point overlooking the sea. Lynne seemed determined to make it the most photographed spot in the universe, making up for all the shots she had missed, and her exaggerated enthusiasm provided them with enough material for good-humored bickering until they reached Gold Beach.

They saw historic Cape San Sebastian, across the rushing Rogue River, breathless miles of rich pine coastland, and Jim infected Kathy and Lynne with his enthusiasm again — sounding as though he were employed by the Oregon Chamber of Commerce and going out of his way to point out the site of one of the last Indian wars at Battle Rock, near Port Oxford, and extolling the scenic virtues of the nearly two hundred campsite parks in his home state. He even succeeded in convincing Kathy that in the presence of a majestic snowcapped mountain, or a placid lake edged with evergreen spires, or the spectacular cascade of Multnomah Falls irritations with people like Ralph Knoll assumed their proper perspective; viewing nature's grandeur had a way of reducing petty human beings to their proper, miniscule size. Knollside Community Hospital was not the world, Jim pointed out.

"Knollside?" Kathy gazed out the car window, drinking in the loveliness surrounding her, at peace with herself for the first time in more than a week. "Knollside, did you say? Never heard of it."

It was perfect. Almost too perfect. And according to Jim's calculations, if he wasn't ordered to make too many camera stops by the shutter-happy blonde at his side, they would be out of Coos Bay and North Bend early enough to make Bayport in time for dinner. "That is, providing no one's starving?" No one was, and he gunned the car forward; a man so completely happy that no one within the sound of his voice could be otherwise.

In spite of not wanting to miss seeing any of the inspiring landscape, Kathy closed her eyes and dozed. Steady purr of the motor, Lynne's head leaning against Jim's shoulder, the radio playing softly . . . a disc jockey spinning ancient pop tunes on Jim's hometown station. Jim was listening avidly, especially to the commercials, punctuating the announcements with, "That's the department store where we shop." Or, "McGrudy's Drugs. I'll be darned! That's the drugstore my dad owned before he died. I grew up in the place!" Then, noticing that Lynne was asleep and Kathy was silent, he contented himself with hamming quietly along with an early Bing Crosby record.

Kathy awoke to hear Lynne saying, "Why didn't you *tell* me we're only a few miles from Bayport? Honey, I wanted a half hour to put my face back together."

"Your face looks fine to me," Jim said.

"Sure, but you're biased!"

"You bet your boots!" Jim threw an arm around Lynne and squeezed her affectionately. "How biased can a guy get?"

"Well, slow down and at least give me a chance to comb my hair." Lynne turned toward the back seat. "Leave it to my boy — let's me meet my future mother-in-law looking like. . . ." She groped around the front seat, apparently looking for her handbag. "Is my purse back there, Kath? I think I left it in the back after we stopped at that gas station."

"It's on the floor," Kathy said, reaching down for the black leather bag. She had closed her hand over its tortoiseshell frame when the cry came from Jim — a short, startled intake of breath. Lynne spun around, and Kathy raised her head in time to see the oncoming vehicle — a tiny red bug of a sports car that must have skidded out of control turning the sharp bend just ahead of them. A split second in which to register the fact that a collision was inevitable, and another instant in which Lynne screamed and grabbed at the wheel as Jim made an abrupt swerve into the opposite lane. And then only a shrieking instant in which the red bug whizzed past them and the big sedan skidded too far across the narrow shoulder, careening wildly over the pebbled surface and plunging over the cliff's edge.

Cries, a brief flash of boulders, surf and sand, then the monstrous crash and thudding impact. And then no sound at all.

six

There was a thin, whining hum in her ears, but that came later. Her first conscious reaction was to the smell. Familiar odor. Not strong, but undeniably there. Medicinal.

Kathy's eyes remained closed, but she inhaled deeply, verifying the faintly recognizable disinfectant smell. She was back on duty. Everything had been straightened out, and she was back at Knollside. Spending too much time in one room . . . the Ice Pick would be wondering why she didn't get around the floor faster . . . so many other patients to be cared for . . . couldn't linger any longer than necessary with. . . .

Abruptly, it came to her that she was not standing beside the bed. She was lying *in* it, her cheek pressed hard against a cool white pillow, her body completely relaxed — except for the sharp pain in her shoulder as she tried to turn over.

It was the pain that awakened her. That, and an awareness that *someone* was standing beside the bed. Not Nurse Barrett. *She* was lying *in* the bed; she would have to remember that. She was lying here, her mind floating, yet conscious of that someone standing over her. Someone. Kathy opened her eyes slowly.

She had seen his face before. And yet she had *not* seen his face before. I'm in a hospital, Kathy told herself silently. I'm in a hospital, and they've given me something to stop my shoulder from hurting, but my mind's all foggy as a result. Otherwise I'd know Jim Stratton when I see him, wouldn't I? Same dark brown hair, same eyes. Trying to smile at me, but not doing too well. White medical jacket. Well, naturally. *Doctor* James Stratton . . . he'd be wearing white. Though, this morning . . . hadn't he been wearing a loud checked sport coat?

He was doing better now with the smile, though his eyes looked — what was the word? Melancholy? Troubled? No, that wouldn't make sense. A few seconds ago . . . when was it? . . . she had thought he must be the happiest man in the world.

She became aware of a dull, aching sensation throughout her body, and, simultaneously, an overwhelming desire to close her eyes once more and sleep. But there was this perplexing problem to solve first. This problem about Jim Stratton looking older. And taller. And more serious, somehow. Kathy stared directly into the familiar-unfamiliar face. "Jim?"

"Jim's not here," he said quietly.

Insane, because now he didn't even *sound* like Jim. Husky, deep voice. Speaking slowly, not in the loud staccato that usually made him sound more like a carnival pitchman than a doctor. But, of course, this was his bedside manner. Of course. Kathy repeated his name, hearing herself now as if she were in some distant echo chamber: *"Jim?"*

"Shh! Easy. Go back to sleep," he said. Jim Stratton telling someone to be quiet! All strange. Everything strange. And strangest of all, proving that they *had* given her a shot of something powerful to stop the hurting shoulder, he said, "Everything's all right, Lynne. Try to sleep."

It was all ridiculous, and for a moment she thought she might burst into laughter. But he kept repeating the words, and a cool, heavy hand was stroking her forehead. *"Sleep, Lynne. You're very tired. Sleep."*

He sounded tired himself. *Looked* tired. Dark circles under his eyes. Sleep now, and tell him later . . . that he had it all wrong. All wrong, because he wasn't Jim Stratton and she wasn't Lynne Haley. Everything . . . all wrong!

Was it minutes later? Hours? Days? Kathy awoke suddenly and completely the second time, blinking her eyes at the daylight. There was someone else standing beside the bed now. A nurse. Older woman — probably about the Ice Pick's age, but heavier, not as steely, her face less harshly lined, though the glasses and thin pink lips were reminiscent of the old head nurse.

"Good morning!" she said cheerfully, with that false cheer cultivated by nurses, and used only when it isn't *going* to be the best kind of morning. *When you've been told to keep the patient relaxed and say nothing about what's happened.*

Kathy's mind seemed acutely alert. She responded to the greeting, remembering in one sweeping, sickening flash the red sports car, the crunching skid of tires on coarse gravel, the terrifying sensation of falling — and then the explosive, ear-splitting crash of metal against rock. "What happened? What about Jim and —"

"Now, you're not to worry about anything, dear." That professionally practical effort at calmness again! "We're going to get cleaned up and have our picture taken. . . . Doctor wants some X rays this morning. And then we'll come back here for a nice breakfast. . . ."

One of those nurses who talked in plurals! "*We*" were going to do this and "*we*" were going to do that! "Please don't treat me like a sheltered child," Kathy said irritably. She was being inexcusably rude, but the fake, almost patronizing, attitude had jarred her nerves, a frightening suspicion tightening like a hard knot under her ribs. "I want to know what's happened!"

"You were very lucky, dear. Minor abrasions. Fractured right scapula . . . don't be disturbed if you try to lift your arm and it hurts here. . . ." The nurse indicated Kathy's right shoulder and upper arm. "We're going to get X rays of it this —"

"Will you tell me what happened to my friends?" Kathy tried to sit up, a jagged bolt of pain throwing her back to the pillow.

Miss whatever-her-name-was looked distressed, glancing uneasily toward the door, then turning away from Kathy momentarily on the pretext of taking a wash basin from the bedstand cabinet. Vaguely, with an unconvincing effort at lightness, she said, "I just came on duty, dear. Your doctor will know more about it, I'm sure. Now, we'll get our face washed. . . ."

"I want *you* to tell me!" Fear sticking in her throat . . . hearing her voice rise to a pitch of hysteria, the way she had heard patients cry out when she tried to lie to them, to keep them from knowing — *knowing what a sixth sense already told them!*

"Please, dear . . . I have to get you ready for —"

"They're . . . dead!"

"You mustn't get yourself upset, dear." *That final, revealing hospital cliché!* "If you want me to, I'll see if I can reach Dr. Stratton. . . ."

"Dr. Stratton?"

The nurse nodded uncomfortably and hurried toward the door. "I'm not sure he's here at the hospital, but I'll see if I can locate him, Miss Haley."

It began to swim in her head then, and something inside her threatened to explode, to shatter the walls with a piercing scream. *Dead!* Lynne and Jim — both of their lives snuffed out. Ecstatically happy in one second, teasing each other playfully . . . arguing back and forth like delirious, joy-filled kids . . . the camera . . . Jim not waking Lynne up in time to make herself pretty for her introduction to her new family . . . and Jim hugging her. Biased. "You bet your boots I am! I'm biased because I love you . . . I love you, and we're going to be married, and in a few more minutes the people closest to me are going to meet you and love you, and then they'll be biased, too . . . even though your hair's not combed and your nose is shiny. . . ."

Lynne . . . oh, Lynne . . . come into the room! Please! Walk in and let me see you — tell me the nurse really DID just come on duty . . . and doesn't know!

A violent sob wracked Kathy's body, but the tears lay hot and leaden inside her. *Lynne! Funny little sister, taking ten pictures of the same rocky beach because Jim wouldn't stop for all the other shots . . . in too great a hurry to stop because he couldn't wait to show you to his family . . . Lynne! Lynne! Lynne, it's too monstrous! Come in and tell me it's a lie! Jim, you tell me! Jim!*

Someone was shouting wild, barely coherent sentences. Someone was calling Jim Stratton's name, sobbing wildly, screaming for him, demanding that he come back — come into the hospital room. . . .

And there were hushed, clipped voices. Other voices. Someone holding her down. Pinning her arm to the bed to keep it from flailing the air. And then the stabbing pain in her shoulder was offset by a quick needle jab into a vein in her left arm.

They're putting me back to sleep, Kathy thought angrily. Putting me back to sleep because they don't think I'm ready to know. But I do! I know everything they're trying to keep from me! *I'll never see Lynne and Jim Stratton again!*

She made a resentful, determined effort to resist the soporific effects of the hypo. They couldn't do this to her! Her best friend dead . . . Lynne gone, Jim . . . their love and all the tomorrows they looked forward to sharing, gone . . . and they wanted her to sleep as though nothing was wrong!

Kathy struggled against the lulling blanket of drugged sleep. Struggled, heard herself crying, again as if from some distant room. And then felt herself drifting . . . experiencing once more the sensation of plummeting downward . . . down . . . down into the bottomless reaches of a black pit in which there was only silence. Remembering only faintly that the bewildered, unprepared nurse had made the same mistake that someone else had made earlier. He — the Dr. Stratton who looked like Jim — had called her "Lynne." The nurse had said, "I'll see . . . I'll see if I can . . . see if I can locate him . . . *Miss Haley!*"

He was back. And because he looked so

miserable and was trying not to let her see beyond his façade of calmness, Kathy bit her lower lip and commanded herself to remain quiet. If she said a word, she would go to pieces again. And it wasn't fair to him, because he was making such a valiant effort to tell her the truth gently. And he *was* telling her the truth, his suffering even greater than hers, because he couldn't *permit* himself to break down — and because Jim Stratton had been his kid brother.

"You mustn't let yourself think about it too much," he was saying huskily. "I know that sounds impossible . . . but I'm asking a favor of you, Lynne."

Kathy moved her head from side to side slowly. "You don't understand. . . ." Tears blotted out the sight of his face and she bit her lip harder. He looked as though he would collapse if she cried. Exhausted and on the verge of collapse.

"It's very important that the two of us keep our chins up," he went on. "I know it's a terrible blow for you. But you've got to get well . . . and you've got to be strong. My mother . . . *Jim's* mother . . . Jim told you my dad's gone . . ."

Kathy nodded, something inside her head spinning.

"That was quite a blow to her. This . . . what happened Saturday . . . has been almost too much. She has a bad heart. About all that's keeping her together now is . . . she's concerned about you: Jim's girl. She keeps saying that she's lost a son, but . . . she has a . . . daughter to look after. If you can hold up, between the two of us, we can. . . ." He released his breath, as though he had given up hope of expressing himself with words.

"There's been a . . . mistake of some kind," Kathy said feebly. "Jim and I weren't —"

"I know you weren't married yet. But you were going to be . . . that's all she cares about."

"Dr. Stratton. . . ."

"Dane. Call me Dane."

"Dane. . . ." The dizziness came over her again — the whirling, black dizziness that came whenever the awesome reality, the terrible finality, penetrated her conscious mind. And she tried to tell him. Tried desperately in a jumble of half-formed sentences. After which, frustratingly, he told her that Kathy Barrett had been identified . . . and that Lynne would be relieved to know that although they had contacted Knollside Hospital. . . .

Words. Something about determining Miss Barrett's identity through a wallet in her handbag . . . and Lynne's from the purse she had clutched in her hand when the ambulance attendants extricated her, unconscious but miraculously alive, from the twisted wreckage. And since it was established that Miss Barrett had no living relatives, arrangements were being made by the Stratton family. . . .

Words, all of them senseless, adding to the unbearable gyrating sensation in her brain. When it stopped, she would tell him. When the room stopped going round and round, creating a nauseous feeling in the pit of her stomach, she would explain to Dane Stratton that . . . his mother couldn't count on her for strength. His mother had lost her "daughter," too. "Lost . . . both of them . . ." she managed to say. "I don't know how you're going to . . . tell her. . . ."

"I'm tiring you," he said gently. "We'll talk again when you're feeling stronger. Meanwhile, keep trying to raise that right arm." Brisk now. Forcing the impersonal, professional tone as a nurse came into the room, carrying a medication tray. His words were apparently intended for someone else. Kathy caught a fleeting glimpse of another R.N. Probably the head nurse;

the room was getting too dark to make out her form. "X rays showed a good position of the glenoid, but there's some apparent extrusion of fragments on the inferior aspect of the neck. I won't prescribe any specific exercise . . . just gradual increase in activity as the patient tolerates it."

A hushed voice said, "Very well, Doctor." A pause, then the same voice whispered, "I think she's asleep, Miss Hutchinson. Don't disturb her, poor thing. We'll paint those abrasions when she wakes up." And, after another pause, "I wish you could get some sleep, Doctor. We know how difficult this has been for you."

"Thank you, Mrs. Borowski."

"Tell your mother . . . we're all terribly sorry. How is she taking it, poor dear?"

"You know my mother."

"Enough courage for ten women, bless her heart. And Petey?"

"Pete's with her, thank goodness. They're holding each other up. None of us can believe it yet."

"I know. I saw Angie at church last Sunday, and all she could talk about was . . . Jim coming home and bringing his sweetheart. Look at her! Isn't she the prettiest thing you ever laid eyes on?"

"Beautiful."

"You go home and look after your mother, Doctor. Tell Angie we're taking good care of her little girl."

"She knows that, Mrs. Borowski."

"She's . . . Miss Haley's not a nurse, is she?"

"No."

"I thought . . . Jim might have met her in that hospital down in California."

"No, she's a schoolteacher."

"Poor little thing."

More words sifting through the mist of fleeting consciousness. People talking, saying things that weren't true. Why couldn't she say something?

Sleep . . . always the whirling, falling, over-the-precipice illusion . . . and sleep. When she awoke, she would tell them that she was, too, a nurse. They would ask her to prove it, because there was that frightful misunderstanding about Lynne's handbag. And she would tell them . . . tell them: "The glenoid cavity is the joint surface . . . of the scapula . . . at the point where it meets the . . . humerus. . . ."

Then maybe they'd understand that they were making a serious mistake, and that she wasn't Lynne Haley. She was. . . .

seven

By the end of Kathy's first four days in Bayport Community Hospital, the horror of her experience, and its tragic aftermath, had become obscured by a strange numbness. A defensive numbness, she suspected. It was no longer necessary to bite her lip or dig fingernails into the palms of her hand to keep from screaming. Unaccountably, it was almost impossible to cry.

During her lucid moments, when she found herself able to analyze what had happened and to examine her own reaction to the accident, she concluded that a trigger mechanism somewhere inside her brain had dropped a curtain, preserving her sanity by blocking out reality. It had happened, and yet it hadn't happened. *"It."* The moment in which life and joy had been transformed instantaneously into death and sorrow was too tenuous to be real. "It" had no place in time. If "it" existed at all, "it" was buried somewhere in the far distant past . . . too long ago to be remembered clearly. Or in the future, because there was no room for "it" in the present; "it" was too horrible to be permitted existence in the present! In some dimly recalled corridor of time, something that she could not, would not, *dared* not accept, had taken place. Kathy's breath accelerated and her heart pounded furiously if she explored that forbidden corridor. And the mechanism would click inside her head, dropping the dense veil that shielded her from agony and truth.

Instead of resenting the efforts to keep her calm and benumbed, Kathy welcomed them now. Mrs. Borowski was protecting her. When a floor nurse appeared at nine p.m. with sleeping pills, Kathy seized them gratefully, hungrily. Sleep was a refuge; it was one of the many escapes from something vague and sinister that must be shunted, covered, buried, in the deepest recesses of her memory.

"Traumatic experience," she heard the nurses whisper. "Shock," they said. "She doesn't realize yet what's happened."

But she knew. Knew and refused to know, just as Mrs. Bailey had known, yet had gone dry-eyed to her husband's funeral. Knowing and not knowing she had helped him escape the pain of staying alive. Observing herself from outside herself, performer and audience rolled into one.

Bayport's nursing staff had evidently been cautioned to keep the patient's mind occupied with pleasant matters and to avoid discussion of the tragedy. They followed their instructions rigidly, and Kathy was appreciative. If they chose to call her "Miss Haley," she lacked the strength to contradict them. Something strange was happening in her mind. Something she recognized only hazily as confused . . . possibly even dishonest. But as long as you rested, moved your arm when they told you to move it, ate your meals when they were served, and closed your eyes when the lights were dimmed, life was tranquil. You could forget what had to be forgotten.

It was only when Dane Stratton came into the room that the inner struggle threatened her. Time and again during his twice-daily visits, Kathy found the ideal moments for obeying a driving compulsion. *Tell him!* She would reach a summit of mental clarity, open her mouth to explain to him simply and logically that she wasn't Lynne Haley at all. She was Kathy Barrett. A nurse. *So* simple and logical and right! And, God knew, he *had* to be told! She would reach the plane of reality and reasoning, and the trigger would release itself. "It" would swallow her up if she spoke. Peaceful and unperturbing to just listen . . . listen to that deep, softly modulated voice. Observe the handsome, serious face. *Close your eyes; lie back and don't spoil everything by thinking . . . talking . . . telling him.*

And it was especially so when Dane talked about his mother. About the coronary attack she had suffered when Mr. Stratton died. About the remarkable stamina she was showing now. "I won't let her up to meet you, Lynne. You'll have to hurry up and get well. Recuperate at home, where the two of you can . . . talk."

At home! Kathy let the words roll luxuriously across her dazed consciousness. *Recuperate at home.*

And though she managed to break through the mental barriers long enough to protest: "I can't move into your house . . . inconvenience you that way!" she said it as Lynne might have said it. Protesting politely. Hoping and knowing the objection would be overruled.

"We want you to stay with us, Lynne. At least until you're on your feet again. Besides, you'll be doing me a great service. You're Mom's replacement for Jim."

Gradually, the bone splinters from her

fractured arm joint became absorbed, the sharp edges and the pain disappearing. And with the physical healing came a third stage, in which there was neither hysteria, nor threat of mental breakdown, nor defense mechanism, nor escape. The tears came freely now, and there was no curtain behind which the truth could be hidden. Two weeks had gone by, and with the recovery of her body came the recovery of her senses. There was no longer any excuse when she didn't interrupt Dane Stratton. When he spoke of her as the girl his brother had loved, there was no reason for not correcting him — no reason that could be tolerated by her conscience.

She had stepped into a cloud-lined trap, from which there was only one escape: admit having lied. Shatter an old woman's hopes that some slender thread still existed, linking her to a dearly loved son. A cardiac case. *Go ahead and tell her Lynne Haley wouldn't be coming to visit because Jim's girl was buried and gone!*

Kathy lay awake long after Dane's evening visits, rationalizing, telling herself she was concerned only about Mrs. Stratton. Concerned about a wonderful old woman, for the same reasons that *he* was concerned.

But there was something else. Something that gnawed at the outer edges of her conscience and came alive whenever Kathy remembered what it would mean to return to Knollside. The now empty apartment, filled with mementos of Lynne. The cavernous rooms, silent, with no promise that Lynne would fill them with laughter or that Jim would fill them with cheerful, clumsy noises. More than that: the hospital. Had they managed to communicate with Mrs. Bailey? And if they had, what had they been able to prove? What if there was no proof? Suspicion might hang over Kathy's head indefinitely. If she were cleared, there would still be Ralph Knoll. There was no returning to Knollside, whatever the results. And if not Knollside, where? Where, when a door was open to her here? Here, where she was not only wanted but also desperately needed? Where else? And *why?*

Her conscience had won the battle. Continuing the innocent misunderstanding was unthinkable. And it could still be interpreted as a mistake, uncorrected because she had suffered a great shock and had been ill. Kathy resolved to tell Dane the truth on the evening before she was to be released. Mrs. Borowski had circled the day on a calendar at Kathy's bedside. December twenty-third. *Home for Christmas!*

Dane didn't come. That was a problem at home, Kathy was told. Mrs. Stratton's stoic reserve had weakened, and Petey had been assigned to visiting duty at the hospital because Dane knew how to bolster his mother's morale.

"All he has to do is keep reminding her that you're coming home tomorrow," Pete Stratton said.

Kathy explored the boy's eyes. He bore little resemblance to his older brothers; apparently he favored a different branch of the family. But he combined Jim's enthusiasm with Dane's level-headedness, so that Kathy would have recognized him as a Stratton if she had met him in the street as a stranger. He hadn't recovered from the shock of his older brother's death, and there were moments when he lapsed into a brooding, introspective silence. Most of the time, however, a boyish enthusiasm emanated from him. "Lynne" would be crazy about Bayport, once she got out of the hospital and could be "shown around." Did she like beachcombing? He could show her some spots where driftwood piled up . . . beautiful gnarled pieces . . . he'd make a driftwood lamp for her room; would she like that? There was a terrific inland lake nearby. Would her arm give her too much trouble if he and Dane took her sailing? "Later on. When things are . . . better at home."

Between his embarrassed silences whenever Jim's name came into the conversation, and his eagerness to impress "Lynne" with the multitudinous assets of living in Bayport, Petey Stratton got across a powerful message. Meeting "Lynne" and welcoming her into the family was a primary issue with his mother. And he, along with Dane, were counting heavily on "Jim's girl" to turn the tide favorably. "She's still got Dane and me — but, see, you're somebody special. She'll be so busy making you feel at home . . . the way we figure, she won't keep thinking about . . . you know."

Kathy lacked the heart to disillusion him. Dane would understand. Dane was an adult, and he would find a way to break the news to Mrs. Stratton. At least . . . he would know what to say. Tomorrow morning, when Dr. Stratton came to sign her release and drive her "home," she would end this unfortunate deception. Tonight. . . .

"Funny thing. You know, when I found out you were a schoolteacher, I thought,

'Oh, *no!*' I figured you were some dried-up prune . . . like, maybe you'd go around giving lectures. No kiddin', I didn't expect you to be — y'know — cute." For the first time since Pete had entered the room, Kathy saw a smile drift across his face. "Don't tell Dane I said that. He'd pin my ears back."

"I won't tell him," Kathy promised. *After tomorrow, I may never see him again. If I weren't dependent upon him for my release, I'd leave the hospital before he arrives. Then I wouldn't have to explain anything to him, either. I'd just disappear . . . save everyone from a lot of embarrassment.*

"Dane's a good Joe, but he rides herd over me like I was a kid or something." Pete didn't look displeased with the situation. "Once I'm in pre-med, he claims he'll scalp me if I go below a B-plus average — and who *doesn't?*" He hesitated. "You aren't interested in medicine, are you?"

"I wouldn't say I'm . . . not interested."

"Personally, I mean. You're kind of squeamish about the subject, aren't you? Don't let it bother you. My Mom's even worse, I'll bet. You two should get along great."

A nurse poked her head into the room to signal the end of the visiting hour. Pete waved her on with an indication that he was on his way. "Miss Velzey," he said. "She's a honey."

"You seem to know everyone here," Kathy observed. He had waved at, or mentioned by name, every staff member who had passed the open doorway.

"I should. I did volunteer work around the place last summer, and sometimes Dane lets me tag along. Anyway, everybody in Bayport just about knows everybody else. I guess that sounds crummy to you . . . coming from a big city."

"No. No, it sounds . . . as though you have a lot of friends."

"Yeah. I guess we have those, all right." Pete looked around the room. "I notice you've got a lot of flowers."

"People keep sending them," Kathy said. "People I don't even know." There were get-well cards, too, piled up on the bedside stand. All of them addressed to Miss Lynne Haley. For a few seconds she entertained a morbid thought. There were probably flowers at Lynne's funeral, too. Ordered by friends of the Strattons — for a stranger named Katherine Barrett!

"The thing is," Pete was saying, "everybody knows *you*. People will be coming over to meet you, and that'll keep Mom occupied, too." He skipped to a more cheerful subject. "Hey, we have a new high school in town, y'know. Is that what you teach? High school?"

Kathy held her breath, but only as long as she dared. If she didn't answer quickly, it would be over . . . the possibility of long, sympathetic conversations with Mom Stratton, the walks along the beach in search of driftwood, the endless procession of interested, understanding friends coming to call! Only that brief hesitancy, and the inner rebellion against deliberate deceit. Then, weakly, knowingly, helplessly — and irrevocably — she closed the door that imprisoned her in the trap. "Not high school," she said. "Kindergarten. I teach kindergarten."

eight

There were no pills powerful enough to induce sleep that last night at Bayport Community Hospital. Kathy lay awake, asking herself how it had been possible to verbalize the deliberate lie: *"I teach kindergarten"!* It was an uncompromising deceit, and she hadn't been dazed or ill or feverish when the words had spilled out of her mouth. What explanation would there be to offer in the morning? In the morning, when Dane Stratton came to "take her home"!

Near dawn, a thin drizzle began to fall, gathering in momentum until the single window in her darkened hospital room ran with rivulets. Exhausted by the raging battle with her conscience, Kathy listened to the pelting rain, watching the patternless formations on the pane. One drop moving downward, blending into another, the added weight hurrying their journey downward . . . faster, to join another and another, gaining speed until, in the reflected glow from streetlights outside the hospital, the connected drops ran like quicksilver and disappeared.

A frightening analogy formed in Kathy's mind. Lies. One running into another, connecting with others, growing in weight and then racing downward. Only downward, with no other course open. A windowpane of lies. Why had she let the first one splatter to start the impossible network of rivers? If she didn't break away now, tomorrow the erratic pattern would expand. More lies, more drops of rain. Running. Always running downhill.

Kathy considered several avenues of escape, but dismissed them, in almost the same instant, as wildly impractical. She had worked in hospitals too long to suppose that she could get out of bed, dress, sneak out of the building undetected, and find her way to a bus depot. In a strange town, in the rain, before dawn! It was a hopelessly melodramatic idea. Leave in the morning, *before* Dane arrived? The dark-green slack suit she had been wearing at the time of the accident wasn't in her closet; two days ago, when Dane gave permission for her to get out of bed, she had looked, finding the closet empty except for her flat-heeled sandals.

Had they found her luggage . . . or Lynne's? Dane had brought the black leather handbag with the wide tortoiseshell frame several days ago, assuming she would want her comb and makeup. Lynne's handbag. The last thing Lynne had requested of her. Kathy had shuddered inwardly . . . yet she had thanked Dane for bringing "her" purse. Another lie; she had forgotten about that one!

Pale, gray daylight filtered into the room and the rain subsided. Kathy closed her eyes, her eyelids heavy, her body aching for sleep. *Don't think. Make a decision and stick to it. The right decision. When Dane comes, ask him to drive you to the bus depot. Tell him you were sick and didn't know what you were saying. Then go back to Knollside. Nowhere else to go. Back to the memory-filled apartment, the hospital, the questioning stares. If they'll have you. If they don't decide that you killed a man!*

Another refrain ran through Kathy's shaky "decision." An endlessly repeated rhythmic counterpoint in four beats: *Home for Christmas . . . home for Christmas . . . home. . . .*

Mrs. Borowski came into the room at seven, determined to supervise the departure personally. "You aren't just another patient, honey," she said. "You're Angie

Stratton's daughter. That's the way we all think of you."

A plump, moon-faced woman in her late fifties, the head nurse wore her colorless hair coiled into a mammoth bun, on top of which her starched cap always managed to sit askew. The effect was one of rakishness, but this illusion was quickly dispelled when she spoke: Mrs. Borowski bathed in sentiment. Not that her often maudlin comments were insincere or that she gloried in tragedy. But when a poignant incident touched her, the poor soul pulled out all the tremolo stops, and sympathy poured from her like a heartrending requiem. This morning she was distraught because Kathy looked as though she had spent a sleepless night.

"Poor little thing. Too nervous to sleep. Why didn't you ring for a nurse? You need your rest, honey."

She went on, Kathy being too nervous to respond intelligently. And, ultimately, Mrs. Borowski got around to the matter of Kathy's "going home" clothes. "Petey brought four suitcases in a while ago. I know this is painful for you, honey, but none of them had name tags . . . the Strattons didn't know . . . and, of course, I wouldn't know which are yours. If you want to tell me what your luggage looks like, I won't bring the other pieces in. I don't want you going home all upset. It's bad enough the night staff didn't see that you got your rest. . . ."

It would be unthinkable to open one of Lynne's suitcases, let alone pretend that the clothes, identical in size with Kathy's own, belonged to her. This was a final warning; if the masquerade weren't ended here and now, problems like this would continue to plague her.

Yet Kathy found herself wondering if someone had already opened all of the luggage — and had seen the lovely white negligee in Lynne's larger bag . . . the new clothes, obviously a trousseau, the frothy lingerie. And what if someone had contrasted that with Kathy's hastily thrown-together last-minute selections? *This was the time to make the break. Tell this understanding old angel of mercy with the tipsy cap! Tell her you couldn't bear to face Dane Stratton. You can count on this woman to help you.*

"I know," Mrs. Borowski was murmuring. "I know how you feel, darling, don't think I don't. You're a sensitive little thing and this has been a terrible strain." She grew more animated then, telling Kathy, "I called on Angie Stratton last night and told her how sweet you are. I could tell she felt better just talking about you. Doctor won't let her up yet — he's such a conscientious man — but the four of us sat there thinking how wonderful it would be if you decided to make your home here in Bayport. First time Angie's brightened up since the funeral. Oh, and Petey . . . that boy can't say enough for you. Oh, here, you were going to tell me about your suitcases."

Kathy described her own. She could never summon the audacity to wear clothes that Lynne had purchased for a honeymoon trip. Nor could she run now. Someone was waiting for her to ease a terrible hurt. She had gone too far, and the promise had been made. There was no choice now except to keep it.

Kathy was dressed in a beige knit casual — her own — when Dane Stratton came to tell her that she was released. If he shared her nervousness, there were no visible signs of it; there was a strong, dependable, Rock of Gibraltar steadiness about everything he said and did, whether he was writing a prescription, helping you into a two-year-old Ford station wagon, inviting staff members to continue their acquaintance with "Lynne" by calling at the house — or looking deep into your eyes when he spoke to you. He was clearly a man who believed in himself, and in those around him; a doctor you trusted instinctively, a man you admired at first sight. How long, Kathy wondered, how long could she look back into those honest, steady eyes without flinching?

Although the rain had stopped, the sky was heavily overcast and fog had settled in low spots along the main street. As Dane guided the station wagon through the almost deserted thoroughfare, an occasional new patch of fog swirled in from the beach west of town. Tinsel Christmas decorations arched the streets in the shopping district, bedraggled by the night rain. In the dismal light, Bayport should have looked drab. Especially since most of its buildings had stood up against salty winds and heavy downpour for at least fifty years. . . .

Bayport should have struck Kathy as a depressing, colorless, dull little burg; one of those towns people hurry through at night en route from one city to another, without a passing glance. And since Dane's conversation was restricted to solicitous questions, asking "Lynne" if she were comfortable, there was no attempt made to praise the town's virtues. In spite of this, Kathy stared into the sleepy residential side streets with a choking sense of home-coming; these were the streets conjured up in wishful childhood daydreams — her ten-year-old concept of a home town, where you lived with a family and everyone you met knew your name. White frame houses, no two exactly alike . . . cupolas and balustrades and yawning porches. People sat on those porches on summer nights, she guessed, exchanging idle gossip and waiting for the ice cream man to pass.

And the trees! Ancient trees, none of which she recognized, because the grounds at the orphanage had offered the shade of one spindly eucalyptus in an asphalt forest, and she had been too busy, since then, studying for and practicing her profession, to acquaint herself with things that grew from the soil. But, oh, the trees — richly green, still rainwater fresh, a deep contrast against the neatly hedged lawns!

Then the unpretentious stores, uncursed by sterile, supermarket efficiency. One grocery store they passed might almost have boasted an old-fashioned pickle barrel, though here and there Kathy noted that chromium, plastic, and progress had made their inevitable inroads.

She saw Bayport once through the eyes of her little-girl longing, and once through the eyes of a little-boy-grown-up — a boy who hadn't made it all the way home: Jim, listening eagerly to the two-man Bayport radio station just to hear these familiar names . . . Overton's Family Shoe Store . . . Myra's Ladies' Apparel . . . McGrudy's Drugs. . . .

Dane broke his silence as they passed the corner drugstore and started to turn into one of the residential streets. "My dad used to own that store. You can still see where the sign's painted over. . . ."

Kathy's eyes were too misty to see the Stratton name on the protruding signboard. "Jim told me about it," she said softly. "I didn't see —"

"Well, don't turn around, Lynne. No sudden tugs on that arm."

Kathy was looking ahead, into the wide, tree-lined avenue. Overhead, the branches of the trees touched to form a green and gray archway.

"I haven't been much of a guide, have I?" Dane said. "Jim used to sell the town to visitors. Petey's like that, too. I guess I . . . like to let people discover things for themselves. You either like a place or you don't."

"Do you?" Kathy asked. "If you had your choice —"

"I *have* my choice," Dane said quietly. "I'm very contented here. Small hospital, but an excellent one. Town's not so small that it's boring, not so crowded that you don't have elbow room. I like it here. I guess Jim couldn't see the kind of future he wanted for himself in Bayport. He wanted to specialize, as you know. I'm a born G.P." He turned toward Kathy. "General Practitioner."

Kathy nodded; even a queasy schoolteacher knew what a G.P. was.

As long as they kept talking, she was less aware of the fear that had settled in her stomach as they turned into Beach Street. They couldn't be far from the house now; Dane had said he lived only a few miles from the hospital. "It's a beautiful little town," she told Dane. "I can understand why you'd want to stay."

"We'll show you around when you're up to it. Though . . . I don't know." Dane's forehead wrinkled and he spoke hesitantly. "Everything here is going to remind one of us about Jim. For instance, we played baseball in this street when we were kids. You won't be able to avoid being reminded, and I'm not so sure it's a good idea. One school of thought tells you to get as far as possible from . . . ghosts. Others run the grief out of their system by looking at it squarely." In his solemn, straight-from-the-shoulder manner, he asked, "What do you think, Lynne? Tell us how we can make it easier for you."

"I . . . don't know," Kathy stammered. "It's . . . too soon to know."

"Frankly, if I were you, I'd get as far away as possible and try to forget. If that's what you want, say the word and I'll arrange it. For selfish reasons, though, I'm hoping you'll stay awhile."

"Selfish reasons?"

"I told you how important you are to my mother."

For a split second it had sounded as though Dane Stratton wanted her to stay in Bayport because. . . .

Dane turned the station wagon into a wide concrete driveway. "This is it," he said simply. "We're home."

Kathy's heart had started to pound. The Stratton house looked exactly as Jim had described it, a rambling two-story frame affair, with wings and porches jutting out haphazardly, yet blending into the latticework trellises and thick, informal landscaping as though it had sprung up out of the ground long ago, when the giant trees growing in the parkway were young. It had been recently painted; in sunlight its whiteness would dazzle the eye. Nothing funereal here to indicate that the residents had suffered a recent and shocking loss; a red-ribboned holly wreath almost covered the front door, and through the wide bay window at the front, Kathy glimpsed a decorated Christmas tree.

Then Dane was helping her out of the car, and Petey Stratton was clomping down the wide wooden stairway, looking younger in jeans and a white sweat shirt than he had appeared slicked up for his hospital visit. He hurried toward them, as noisy and unsubdued as Jim had been. Was it only two weeks ago? "Hi, Lynne! Hey, you look great . . . want me to carry the stuff in, Dane? Ella wants to know if you want breakfast, Lynne? Did you have breakfast yet?"

Pete's unwitting boisterousness saved her. If there had been a hushed, tragic atmosphere as she walked up those steps, she would have turned and fled. Thanks to the flurry of excitement created by Pete, there was barely enough time or silence to breathe a silent plea for forgiveness. (*Lynne . . . you'd understand. You, of all people, you'd know why I'm here. It should have been you . . . I'd give anything if it could have been you! Understand. Please understand!*)

Dane pushed the door open. The elaborate wreath swung back and forth like a fat pendulum. "I told Pete to hang that thing in a more logical place," Dane said. "He goes all out with the decorations. Lights are strung up all around the roof, did you notice?" Then, as though the fact needed to be pointed out, he explained, "He did that nearly three weeks ago."

Petey came jostling behind them, a suitcase in each hand. "Would you rather we didn't light the place up at night, Lynne? Some people might think . . . you know. Business as usual. Like we didn't care. But, see, the way I figure . . . we jazzed the place up for you and Jim. . . ." He stopped abruptly, looking to his older brother as they entered a cozy, old-style vestibule. "Put my foot in it, huh? Sorry, Lynne, if I said the wrong thing."

"You didn't, Petey," she told him gently.

Dane set down the luggage he had carried into the house. In that slow, thoughtful manner Kathy had learned to associate with him, he said, “Just because we’ve had a rough break doesn’t mean we don’t wish everybody else a merry Christmas.”

Pete dropped his burdens to the floor clumsily and closed the door.

“Lynne Haley” had come home.

nine

It was warm inside the Stratton house. A log crackled cheerfully in the huge fireplace, throwing its heat over a long living room in which the already crowded overstuffed furniture had been rearranged to make room for the outsized Christmas tree.

Everything looked as if it had been lifted out of Kathy's imagination and placed here to welcome her; the thick hand woven rugs, the rows of framed photographs on the mantle, the fruit bowl and lace tablecloth on a large circular table in the dining room across the entry hall. No modern decorator would have given it his stamp of approval, and considering Dane's comparatively successful practice, every item in each of the rooms could have been replaced with something more fashionable. But every stick of furniture, every corny decorative touch, looked exactly right somehow. *The Strattons live here,* the rooms said. *Come in and make yourself at home.*

A thin, hatchet-faced, middle-aged woman peered out from a doorway in the dining room — a doorway that Kathy assumed led to the kitchen.

"Ella's dying of curiosity," Pete confided in a loud whisper. "Mom's given strict orders that she gets to meet you first."

"Ella," Kathy repeated.

"Yeah. Dane hired her to help Mom. She's got a thing about ashtrays and pipes. Keeps hiding the darn things where Dane can't find them."

"Shall we go up?" Dane asked.

"We'd better, or Mom'll come down," Pete said.

Kathy's legs began to tremble, and Dane must have noticed, because he cupped her elbow, supporting her as they climbed the staircase. "You're still a little weak. I'll want you to go easy for a few days."

Halfway up the stairs, Kathy stopped. She felt faint and dizzy, the brief sensation of warmth and welcome suddenly erased by a clear realization of what she was doing. Would the shock of learning that Jim's girl had died with him be more devastating *now* . . . or when this fraud had been exposed? *I must have been out of my mind! I can't do this to these people!*

"Lynne?"

"I . . . *can't!*"

Dane's hand tightened on her arm.

"Easy! You won't break down, Lynne. Is that what you're afraid of?"

Pete was behind him on the stairway, asking, "Is she okay, Dane? Maybe she oughta lie down. You all right, Lynne?"

They were worried about her. But they were concerned about Mrs. Stratton, too, Kathy guessed. If she collapsed now, told them she had come into their home as an imposter, they would hold her responsible for the effect upon their mother. Kathy forced herself to climb the remaining stairs. "I'm all right. A little tired, I guess."

Dane guided her to the end of an airy hallway papered with a pink cabbage-rose design, Pete still tagging behind them.

I don't deserve to have her like me! They'd all hate me if they knew . . . and they would have loved you, Lynne . . . loved you. . . .

Dane opened the door and ushered Kathy into the bedroom. "Lynne's here, Mom," he said quietly.

Kathy had expected to find Mrs. Stratton in bed. She was seated in a big rose-colored wing chair next to the ruffle-curtained windows, a blanket over her knees. She was tiny. There was room in the wing chair for two like her. And at first glance she appeared frail. Then you looked beyond the pale, fragile features, the feathery halo of white hair, and you saw in her dark eyes the same resolute strength that was reflected in Dane's. You sensed that in a moment of crisis, rather than clutching your arm in terror, she would offer her own to sustain you.

Kathy moved forward a step or two — awkward, not certain what was expected of her.

Dane completed the introduction. "Lynne, this is Mom." As simply as that.

And what was there to *say?* Kathy stared at the beautiful older woman dumbly. A formal "How do you do?" or "I'm happy to know you?" How could she, when neither Jim's mother nor his "girl" could think in terms of being happy at this crucial moment?

Mom Stratton was studying her with those soft, gentle, yet penetrating, eyes. In another second she might say something heartbreaking and Kathy dreaded her own reaction. *I'll be too ashamed to go on with it. I'll burst into tears and tell her!*

It seemed that minutes had ticked by in awesome silence, yet it was only a matter of seconds before Mom Stratton said, "You're as pretty as he said you were, Lynne." Pleasant, with no trace of tears in her surprisingly young voice. Nothing of

Mrs. Borowski's cloying sentimentality. And presumably she was referring to Jim's letter when she paid the compliment, but she didn't mention his name. *Out of consideration for me,* Kathy thought.

It was natural, after that, to lean forward and kiss Mom Stratton's forehead. Natural, too, to find herself kneeling at the feet of this long-sought mother figure, her head against the blanket. Crying softly — knowing that Jim's mother was crying, too — and a soothing old hand petting her hair. Natural and necessary, all of it.

A long time later, Kathy raised her head. Dane and Petey were gone.

"We needed a good cry," Mom Stratton said. She reached to take a clean tissue from the low table beside her chair, blew her nose, then patted the tissue box. "Help yourself, Lynne. We can't go downstairs looking all . . . bloated."

Kathy got up to blot her eyes. She felt at ease with Mom Stratton now. Even hearing herself called "Lynne" hadn't jarred her this time. "What's all this about going downstairs, Mrs. Stratton?"

"Mom."

"Mom."

"Or Angie. My name's Evangeline, if you can believe anything that absurd." She smiled, looking up at Kathy as though she expected the smile to be returned.

"I can believe it. My —"

Kathy caught her breath. She had come close to saying that her middle name was Arvella . . . and wasn't *that* more outlandish than Evangeline? She would have to be careful. Every moment, for as long as she remained in this house, she would have to weigh every word. Talk like Lynne, think like Lynne . . . *be* Lynne. "My best friend's middle name was Arvella."

"You were close friends, I imagine?"

Kathy nodded, feeling the blood rushing to her temples.

"We won't talk about it now," Mom Stratton said. "You were asking me about my going downstairs. That's exactly what I *am* going to do. I'm not any good to myself or anyone else cooped up in here. It's different with you. You're just out of the hospital, and if Dane says you need rest, you rest, dear."

"He's concerned about. . . ."

"My heart. Nothing wrong with my heart that going downstairs and fixing dinner wouldn't cure. You get outnumbered by men, and they want to order you around." She was beginning to sound more and more like the Ice Pick, except for the soft, youthful quality of her voice. "Think a medical degree gives them leave to tell you how *you're* feeling. We have to humor them along, dear, but there's a limit. Ella's a fine person. Best cleaning woman in town. But, you know, she can't cook."

"Can't she?" The reminiscent complaints sounded nostalgically familiar. And hearing Mom Stratton display an interest in what went on around her was immensely satisfying. *She knew what she needed,* Kathy thought. *"A good cry" — and the companionship of a woman who shared her grief. Lynne. Lynne Haley.*

". . . doesn't know how to boil an egg," Mom was saying. "I don't know how the boys have survived with me out of the kitchen." And as if that statement weren't sufficiently typical of the wiry head nurse at Knollside, she added, "The thought of Ella making Christmas dinner! You ought to taste her mashed potatoes. *Lumpy.* She adds the milk cold. Isn't that disgraceful?"

"Disgraceful," Kathy echoed.

"We're going to get along fine, you and I. Now be a dear and call downstairs. Tell Petey to show you your room. I expect he's brought your things upstairs by now: I heard him dropping suitcases."

"All right."

"And have him tell Dane I'm coming downstairs for lunch. Then you lie down and have a nice rest. We'll have plenty of time to visit later."

Surprisingly, Dane didn't oppose his mother's decision. In the rose-bedecked hallway, as Petey escorted Mom Stratton downstairs, Dane touched Kathy's forearm. "Thanks," he said.

"For?"

"For replacing Jim. You've made her as happy as she can possibly be under the circumstances."

"She's a courageous woman, Dane."

"Keeps the things that hurt inside herself, you mean. That doesn't preclude shock." Dane's face lighted up with an affectionate half-smile. "You're better than digitalis or adrenalin."

Lynne would have frowned and asked for definitions. Kathy compromised by looking bewildered. There was no turning back now.

"Heart stimulants," Dane explained.

"I see."

"Petey's shown you your room?"

"Yes. It's very pretty."

"Never mind the decor. Get into bed. I'll have Ella bring your lunch upstairs."

"I don't think it'll be —"

"Scoot!"

"Yes, Doctor."

Dane smiled and started for the stairway, turning around before Kathy had a chance to open her door. "You sound more like a nurse than a patient," he said. "They have a way of saying that 'Yes, Doctor.' Sort of a reflex response."

He was on his way down the stairs and there was no need to supply an explanation.

Kathy added the automatic reply to doctor's orders to a growing list of *don'ts*. She wouldn't remember them all. You had to be a good liar to pretend you were someone else. And assuming you succeeded, how long could you go on, when you despised yourself for your skill at lying?

It was wrong — rotten and shameless and cruelly wrong. Yet the cool, sweet scent of the forget-me-not-papered bedroom, and the warm glow that had come with being accepted by the Strattons, soothed her blistering conscience. She had been of value to Mom Stratton. Dane and Petey had let her know they were glad she had come into their home. And Lynne wouldn't have begrudged her this taste of belonging.

Kathy stretched herself across the chenille-covered bed, amazed to discover, when a curious woman named Ella knocked on the door and carried in an abominable lunch, that she had slept soundly for more than three hours.

ten

They performed the rituals of Christmas without pretending a false holiday gaiety that none of them felt. Kathy's admiration for the Strattons grew, seeing the way they neither forgot their tragedy nor let it throw a morbid pall over their lives. Life went on. Their love for Jim had been so strong that now they felt no need to dramatize it with prolonged, official mourning. Jim would have behaved the same way had the circumstances been reversed. It was a Stratton trait, and grief was a private affair.

Near the end of the week, before they had seen the New Year in, friends and neighbors who had bided their time out of respect for the family's privacy began to appear at the door in increasing numbers. There seemed to be no one in Bayport who didn't admire Angie Stratton, respect her sons, and look forward to meeting "Jim's girl."

Kathy grew accustomed to being introduced as Lynne Haley, sharing the companionable visits with Mom Stratton,

Petey, and sometimes Dane. The holidays hadn't changed his schedule; he was as freely available, as unhesitatingly "on call," as a nineteenth-century horse-and-buggy doctor in the backwoods. In spite of the parade of sympathizers, well-wishers, and generally interested friends, Kathy noticed that the house seemed empty without Dane. She found herself watching for the flash of headlights as he turned his station wagon into the driveway. She became alert and somehow more vibrantly alive when he stepped into the hall.

There were hours alone when the very thought of her unbelievable pose filled her with stark terror. And there was that close brush with exposure when the local elementary school principal engaged her in a discussion about audiovisual procedures in the primary grades. Kathy remembered enough phrases from conversations with Lynne to escape detection. The man even hinted broadly that Bayport's population was growing, and that several new teachers would have to be hired before the fall semester; would Miss Haley be interested?

"I don't think I'll be here that long," Kathy explained. "I should report back on the second of January."

He was curious to know about "Lynne's"

school in Knollside. Over her head in the academic shoptalk, Kathy invented a chore that required her immediate attention in the kitchen. Did the principal look suspicious, or was it only guilt feeding her imagination? *Drops of water on a windowpane!* There was nothing for her to do in the kitchen, but how quickly one lie joined another and another!

There were other moments of panic: coming down for breakfast in the morning to see Dane talking with two policemen. (What was the penalty for false impersonation?) The officers, it developed, were only interested in securing a few missing details about the accident. Now that Miss Haley was feeling better, could she possibly recall anything that would help them trace the party responsible? Kathy explained that the red sports car had been going so fast that the driver had probably whizzed by without even knowing he had forced the Buick off the road. No, she hadn't seen the license plate. No, she couldn't tell them the make of the car. Chances of finding it, even if she recognized the model, were one in a million, but there were records to complete. . . .

"I'm sorry we had to bother you, Miss Haley," one of the officers said. He had undoubtedly noticed that Kathy's hands were shaking uncontrollably. Afterward, it took most of the morning before she could draw a deep breath.

And there was the brief discussion on New Year's Eve, after Mom Stratton had gone to bed — Petey starting it off by asking Dane if he would be going to Knollside the day after tomorrow.

"Knollside?" Kathy repeated. Again that feeling that the air had suddenly turned cold and had frozen in her lungs.

"Unpleasant matters," Dane said evasively.

Petey jumped in to explain that Jim's business affairs would have to be settled. There was the problem of selling his office equipment or turning his entire practice, offices, etc., over to another doctor. His apartment had to be closed, and his personal effects disposed of. He had kept his living quarters, planning to return to them with his bride.

"You might want to make these decisions, Lynne," Dane said. "Or would it be too rough on you?"

"I don't think I'd . . . be able to do it," Kathy said. But she visualized Dane in Knollside: talking to Jim's friends at the hospital, piecing together bits of conversations and descriptions — and coming back to Bayport knowing the truth.

Until then, the possibility of Dane's going to Knollside hadn't occurred to her. And now the subject opened to include "Lynne's" future plans. If she were going to stay, she would have to notify "her school." And give up *her* apartment. Would she be up to driving down with Dane in a day or so?

The picture of herself returning to Knollside with Dane Stratton threw her into a panic. She *couldn't* go back now! *With or without Dane, she couldn't ever go back!* By now, everyone in Knollside "knew" that Kathy Barrett had been killed! Everyone — the apartment manager, the Ice Pick, casual acquaintances, Mr. Anderson, Ralph Knoll!

Petrified by the complications that hadn't crossed her mind during those dazed, confusing hours in the hospital, Kathy clenched her fists, on the verge of screaming.

"We shouldn't be talking about these things in front of you," Pete said apologetically. "Listen, Lynne, you forget all the details. Dane can handle them."

"I'm hoping I can get away," Dane said. From what Kathy had seen of his schedule, taking a week off from his practice seemed impossible. And it would take at least a week, Dane figured. Two days of driving, and heaven only knew how long to settle Jim's estate. "I have patients to think about. Every other doctor in town has a jammed schedule. I can't ask anyone to take over while I'm gone."

Kathy's blood pressure mounted. Another devastating thought had swept over her. If Kathy Barrett no longer existed, she couldn't ever again practice as a nurse. How was she going to earn a living? *I was insane! I should have thought of these things! If I tell them now, what's it going to do to Mom Stratton? If I don't, I'm finished as a nurse — finished being ME!*

Pete was saying something, mentioning a name. And Dane was tapping his pipe inside an ashtray at his side and saying, "Why didn't I think of that? Larry! He'd be the logical person!"

Kathy managed to hold her nerves together until their conversation disclosed that Larry Forbes, a second cousin who practiced law in San Francisco, would know more about settling Jim's unfinished business than Dane. An attorney, a relative — he had been in New York on business the day of the funeral, but he had always been fond of Jim. Lived less than thirty miles from Knollside. . . .

"I'll phone him tomorrow," Dane said. "You've got a head on your shoulders, Pete."

"Sure I have. And look, Lynne could wire her school, couldn't she? Tell them she's quitting?"

"I can't . . . quit my job," Kathy blurted out. (Insane! Could she go back to Knollside and teach in Lynne's classroom?)

"Let's let *her* decide what she wants to do," Dane said evenly.

Pete, encouraged by his inspired idea about their attorney relative, seemed prepared to tackle any problem that arose. "She doesn't want to go back there . . . all by herself! She likes it here. Mom wants her to stay. *We* do. So why couldn't she find a job in Bayport if she wants one? Anyway, you said she's not up to it yet. Can't lift her arm all the way. . . ."

"I'm not trying to make her feel unwelcome," Dane pointed out. "Lynne knows better. But we don't force people to do something they don't want to do, just because it's more pleasant for us."

"You know how Mom would feel if —"

"It's Lynne's decision," Dane said firmly.

"Okay, okay. I just thought . . . see, if she let the people who own her apartment know, they could get someone to pack everything and ship it here. Larry could arrange that, couldn't he? She wouldn't have to go back at all."

It could be done Pete's way. It could. And the problems of how to earn a living, of how to refuse a teaching job for which she wasn't qualified, of how to get back into nursing — all that could be figured out later. Wait until Mom Stratton was feeling stronger, go to another city . . . write to Mr. Anderson, explaining the mistake . . . begin all over again somewhere.

The future wouldn't be free of troubling decisions. But the present, at least, would gain some semblance of security if she followed Pete's suggestions.

"I can't . . . sponge off you indefinitely," Kathy said.

Pete made a disgusted face. "Cut that out, Lynne. You're . . . like part of the family, right, Dane?"

"I'd like to think so." And before Kathy could wonder if Dane's words hadn't been tinged with the faintest note of sarcasm, he said, "Then it's settled? I'll call Larry and you'll contact your school and the landlord?"

Pete didn't wait for Kathy's reply. "Hey,

this is great. Talk about a New Year's present for Mom! She was telling me this afternoon that she'd just about die if you left, Lynne. When Dane's out and I'm at school, this place gets kind of empty. She'd start brooding. . . ."

Dane glanced at his watch and got to his feet. "I'll make some Tom and Jerrys." It was his way of telling Pete that they weren't going to stir up memories or ghosts, even though it was close to midnight. They knew what to do now, and the subject was closed.

Pete was exuberant. "You mean I get to have a genuine, on-the-level drink? *Me* — a mere minor?"

"Don't let it go to your head," Dane said as he crossed the dining room. "I'm holding yours down to one shake of nutmeg."

They were silent when Dane returned with the steaming mugs, not mentioning the absent member of the family who had brought them together, but strangely aware of him as they waited for sirens outside to signal the end of one year and the arrival of the next.

Kathy alone was conscious of another presence — Lynne's!

A church bell clanged and someone in

the neighborhood fired a series of shots.

"Lynne." Dane raised his cup. "Petey."

Kathy's cup trembled in her hand as she lifted it from the table.

"To a . . . *better* new year," Dane said hoarsely.

Pete didn't finish his special-privilege, "genuine, on-the-level drink." He drank enough to observe the toast and then mumbled something about being tired and thinking he'd go to bed. Neither Dane nor Kathy embarrassed him by looking up as he hurried out of the room; seventeen-year-old males weren't supposed to cry.

A long time later, Dane said, "He looked up to Jim a lot more than to me. Jim went out and *did* things."

"Pete's a lot like Jim was," Kathy observed.

"Yeah. Boisterous, sentimental. Full of life and enthusiasm." Dane sipped at his Tom and Jerry. "I'm the dull, stodgy Rover Boy."

"You're not stodgy. You're not dull, either."

"What do you call being so wrapped up in your work and . . . running a family, that you forget you're a human being?" Dane's self-deprecation wasn't bitter. As always, he was making an objective, undramatic evaluation. "Pete thinks of me as an old codger."

Kathy had wondered, briefly, why there had been no indication of a romance in Dane's life. Understandably, he wouldn't have gone out on dates since her arrival at the house. But among the many visitors, she had expected to meet a local girl in whom he was interested. There hadn't been one, and no significant names had been mentioned by Mom or Pete.

"A kid Pete's age isn't too impressed with an all-work-and-no-play character," Dane continued.

"You're more concerned about what he thinks than —"

"What I'm missing?"

"Yes."

Dane shrugged his shoulders. "Maybe I'm being a hammy martyr. Or, maybe I haven't taken the time to look around." He lifted a corner of his mouth in a facetious grimace. "I expect there's at least one reasonably likable girl in Bayport."

"I'd be willing to bet there are dozens."

Dane shook his head. "Dozens wouldn't intrigue me. You *see* how stodgy I am? One town, one obsession with my work . . . eventually, one girl. If I'm not *really* an old codger by the time she shows up."

There was no rapport, Kathy decided. He was not feeling the tenseness that pervaded the room. More likely he was thinking of "Lynne" as a woman who had loved his brother and was now too immersed in recent memories and shattered plans to be affected by the presence of an attractive, apparently wistful bachelor. Dane was engaging in a platonic exchange with a virtual sister. The breathless, yearning sensation that had replaced Kathy's earlier panic was hers alone. But it was unmistakably there, deep inside her, awakened from a long sleep and flooding her bloodstream with an inexpressible longing.

Dane wouldn't be opening his office tomorrow morning. He would be on call, as he always was, but there would be no need to get up early on New Year's Day. He wanted to talk . . . about his days as an intern, his residency, and after he had hung out his shingle, the time it took to convince Bayport old-timers that he was no longer "Stratton's oldest kid," but a qualified physician. And his future plans for improvements at the hospital. Dane had been one of three local doctors who had conceived, made plans for, and raised funds to build the needed medical facility; it was owned by the community and administered by

M.D.'s. Bayport Community Hospital wasn't handicapped by a Ralph Knoll.

Kathy encouraged Dane to talk about himself, not only because a discussion of her own past was filled with risks and slips of the tongue but also because it seemed that Dane had spent most of his years being concerned with others. His own interests had been secondary, it seemed, until now, when reviewing his own achievements and ambitions revealed that he was anything but "dull." Perhaps he was realizing it himself as he talked. Kathy listened with interest; a multifaceted interest that grew with every hour that passed.

They were both amazed when they discovered it was after three a.m.

"Fine doctor, *you've* got," Dane said as he walked Kathy to the foot of the stairs. "Imagine keeping a patient up this late, bragging about yourself."

"You weren't bragging and I'm not a patient." (*I'm a phony house guest. You'd despise me if you knew what I am!*)

"You're a patient until you can rotate that arm." Professionally, with no thought, Kathy was certain, of the electricity in the touch of his hand, Dane took hold of her forearm, lifting it upward and at the same time pressing sensitive fingers at the shoulder joint. "I expected the X rays to indicate subluxation, but we were lucky. No bone dislocation . . . and I'm not worried about those fragments. Does this hurt?"

"Not much."

He let her go. "Keep trying to raise it a little higher every day."

There was, at least for Kathy, an awkward moment of quiet before he said good night, and then Kathy climbed the staircase alone.

Too many conflicting thoughts and emotions crowded out sleep, and she was wide awake, a long time later, when she heard Dane's footsteps on the stairs and in the hallway, then the opening and closing of his door. She imagined he had been sitting alone in the big living room, dragging on his pipe, maybe downing a nightcap he had mixed for himself. And thinking. There was no way of knowing about what.

eleven

By the middle of January, Kathy had grown almost accustomed to her new situation. Since the Strattons considerately avoided discussing Jim in her presence, there was little likelihood that she would break down or make some glaring error. Besides, she had known Jim; his personality and activities in Knollside were completely familiar to her.

Furthermore, she had not wholly lost her identity. She was still Kathy, but with another name. Since Lynne had been a total stranger to the Strattons, there were only two elements that required caution on Kathy's part: when Dane and Pete got into a medical discussion, it was necessary to feign complete ignorance; and when the subject turned to teaching, it was wisest to find some excuse to leave the room, especially if the conversation sprang from one of Mom Stratton's visitors; she seemed to number every schoolteacher in town among her friends.

Of the two subjects to be avoided, medicine was the most distressing. Pete, eager to finish high school and follow in his brother's footsteps, had a consummate interest in everything that happened at the hospital or in Dane's office. On weekends, or in the evenings when he had finished his homework, he memorized the names, locations, and functions of nerves, veins, bones, and arteries with the same intensity that he threw into everything else, from his basketball team to convincing "Lynne" that she should remain in Bayport. When he clomped about the house, wondering aloud "What the heck is it the quadratus lumborum muscle does?" it was difficult not to tell him that it made bending the spine in a sideward direction possible. Not because Kathy had any desire to show off her knowledge, but because her forced silence reminded her that unless she regained her name, and along with it her education, experience, and necessary documents, she would never again wear the white uniform of which she was so proud. And unless she could do that, her former life had been wasted.

She would wait, Kathy told herself, only long enough to be certain that her departure wouldn't upset Mom Stratton. Yet every day that went by seemed to increase the older woman's fondness for her . . .

and her dependence. Their long, woman-talk conversations, their kitchen projects, and every hour they shared strengthened the bond between them. And Mom had not needed a daughter more than Kathy had wanted the warm camaraderie of a family. Kathy savored the moments, wanting freedom from deceit, yet postponing the inevitable departure. Through the maze of indecisions, she was motivated now by one strong determination. Somehow, Mom Stratton was going to be spared a second shock.

Kathy had made certain that the shock didn't come when her possessions — and Lynne's — were delivered by the trucking firm Larry Forbes had engaged. She had asked Petey to haul the cartons into her room, thanking Mom for her offer to help, but sorting the clothes, papers, and sentimental possessions herself, behind a locked door.

She couldn't bear the thought of destroying mementoes, but she had felt like a criminal, nevertheless, hiding Lynne's college yearbook, photographs, and other incriminating papers in the bottom of her lingerie drawer, along with similar effects of her own. Kathy's graduation class picture and the treasured portrait for which she had posed wearing her pin and white cap for the first time were hidden, too. It was a symbolic burial, not only of Lynne Haley but of Kathy Barrett as well.

Lynne's clothes were repacked in cartons and driven, by Petey, to a collection station maintained by Mom's pet charitable organization.

There was nothing illegal about these maneuvers. It was only when Kathy was forced to forge a signature on Lynne's severance-pay check, that she crossed the line of the law. The check had arrived soon after Kathy had sent a wire advising the Knollside school principal that she would not be back. Her personal expenses were low, but the cash she had withdrawn from the bank before her trip wouldn't last long, especially if she found an opportunity to break away and start anew. The Strattons' insistence that proceeds from Jim's estate be turned over to her raked her conscience. And there was no way to cash a check on her own account in Knollside; Dane had promised to ask the San Francisco attorney what to do about "Miss Barrett's funds," a small amount, but a source of frustration to Kathy now.

Unfortunately, Mom had been present

when Kathy opened the letter accepting her resignation. And she had seen the check. When she mentioned it at the dinner table, Dane had said, "I'm going to the bank in the morning. Endorse it and I'll get it cashed for you." At that point, Kathy had nearly choked on her dessert.

"It's a . . . rather large amount, Dane. I don't want that much cash on hand. Maybe I'll walk over in a day or two and open an account." (She could destroy the check. No one needed to know.)

"Man, that'll make her a resident, won't it?" Pete had said.

And the excuse would have held up, except that it occurred to Kathy that if the check *weren't* put through the bank, there might be questions asked at the other end. A few days later, disgusted with herself, she copied Lynne's free-flowing signature, let Petey drop her off at the bank on his way to Bayport High, and opened a checking account for "Lynne Haley."

If her masquerade was discovered now, the consequences would be legal as well as emotional. Yet, of the two, Kathy dreaded Mom's tears and Dane's revilement more than a possible arrest.

With painful necessities disposed of,

Kathy began to sample the sweeter fruits of her deception.

There were long evenings when Dane wasn't at the hospital or on a house call — long evenings after Petey had retired to his room with algebra homework and Mom had gone to bed — when all of the agonies Kathy had precipitated with that first lie seemed justified. When they talked, she would resent the moving hands of the clock, hating the moment when she would be separated from the sound of that deep, quiet voice. All that there was to know about him, she wanted to know. And there were moments — brushing against him accidently while they fixed a midnight snack in the kitchen, or when he leaned over her shoulder while showing her architect's drawings for the new hospital wing — when she would have sworn that only the ghost of a man she had supposedly loved separated them. A man didn't take a woman into his arms knowing that only a few weeks ago she had lost the man with whom she had wanted to spend the rest of her life. Dane didn't. But the intuitive sense that he wanted to pounded in her pulse.

Nor did it strike Kathy as incongruous when she admitted to herself that she was in love with Dane Stratton. She had waited for him all her life. Living with him as closely as she did, it was more amazing to her that it had taken nearly a month to make the discovery — and to add that love to the heaven and hell on earth she had created for herself.

"You're missing your calling, Petey. You might make a good doctor, but you'd be a *fabulous* salesman."

It was a Saturday morning late in January, and they were driving home from the grocery store in Pete's jalopy. Kathy had been listening to his description of a state park at which a family outing had been planned for the next day. Not even Jim Stratton had painted Oregon's woods, mountains, and beaches with a more colorful brush.

"Okay, so I'm exaggerating. You'll see. The water's like crystal, except when you get to the lake, you think it's bright blue, clean down to the bottom. The fishing. . . ." Pete turned into Beach Street as though he were piloting a fire engine, and Kathy's body pressed flat against the old crate's door. "Oh, sorry. I took that one too sharp. Your arm okay?"

"Fine, but take it easy." It wasn't necessary to remind Pete why; even a minor accident to one of Mom Stratton's family might produce a serious reaction.

"Well, like I was saying, the fishing's *fantastic*. Boy, I hope Dane can go tomorrow. Last time we planned to go, he had one of his unscheduled babies. . . ."

For the first time since the accident, Kathy laughed, and Pete joined her, blushing furiously, and then launched into an even more garbled recitation about how Dane usually knew when he'd be free to go fishing on Sunday, but how you couldn't train babies to arrive on weekdays.

He was hopelessly entangled in a description of an obstetric table, and almost within sight of the Stratton house, when they heard the scream.

Pete's head spun around in the direction of the sound. "Hey, look — across the street!"

He pulled the jalopy over to the curb and slammed his foot against the break, leaping out of the car in almost the same motion, Kathy getting out only seconds after him.

"What's the matter?" he was yelling as he ran across the street. "What's wrong, Peg?"

Kathy had barely had time to see the girl

from the car. A youngster of about ten, she had been standing on the sidewalk, waving her arms hysterically when they turned toward that first terrified cry. Now, as Pete and Kathy ran toward her, she was kneeling down, looking as though she might be shaking a rag doll — except that her frightened sobs made it obvious that the tiny figure lying on the sidewalk was a child.

"That's the Rossiters' kid! What's the *matter* with him, Peggy?"

Kathy had caught up with Pete by then, dropping down beside the child. He was no more than two. And from the bluish color of his face and his strangled attempts to breathe, Kathy realized instantly that he was choking. Without hesitating, she swept her index finger around the inside of his mouth and around the back of his throat without finding any foreign object.

Still, the girl was sobbing something about "a wheel."

". . . the little wheel . . . he got it off his jeep . . . I was supposed to watch him . . . I only left him *one* minute!"

It didn't take a second to deduce what had happened once Kathy's eyes found the toy plastic jeep turned upside down on the grass at her left. One of the hard rubber wheels was missing; it was an object large enough to completely obstruct the passage of air.

"Pete, grab his ankles! Turn him upside down — quick!"

Petey evidently knew more about medical terms than first aid. He hesitated.

"Quick!" Kathy ordered.

Startled by the strength of her command, Pete obeyed, gripping the lower portion of the boy's legs and suspending him in the air, head downward, while Kathy slapped the child's back.

Their efforts failed to dislodge the foreign object.

"Let's get him to the hospital," Pete cried. "I can have him there in —"

"Traffic's too heavy . . . Saturday morning . . . it'd take —"

"Ten minutes." Pete's face dripped perspiration. "Maybe seven."

"Put him down, Pete."

"Huh?"

"Put him down on the grass! We don't have seven minutes! We don't even have *two!*"

The boy's face had turned a deep, telltale blue, and the girl named Peggy increased her sobs. "His mother went to the store . . . nobody's home . . . I was supposed to *watch* him!"

(*When it is obvious that death will otherwise ensue — and ONLY if a doctor is not immediately available —*)

Kathy took a deep breath. "Pete, give me your jackknife!"

"Lynne, you don't know anything about —"

"Hand it to me! *Now!*"

Pete reached into his pocket and gave her the knife reluctantly. He must have guessed, by then, what she was going to do, sucking in his breath loudly as she pulled the blade open with her thumbnail.

The girl had started to shriek, "Don't stab him! Don't hurt him!" In another second Kathy would be completely unnerved by these cries.

"Get her out of here, Pete!"

"Lynne!"

"Do as I say! I know what I'm doing!"

Pete took the girl's arm, leading her toward the house, afraid to go and afraid to stay. Kathy dug her teeth into her lower lip, the girl's tormented cries still piercing her ears.

(*ONLY when it is obvious that death will ensue, perform an emergency tracheotomy.*)

Her textbook instructions had said nothing about failure because your hand was unsteady, or because you had only watched this operation under surgical conditions, never having performed it on a child — a child who was no longer struggling to breathe.

She held the knife poised for only an instant, establishing the tiny lump of the child's Adam's apple with her left hand. Then, biting deeply into her lip, she made an incision in the boy's windpipe at a point below the fingers of her left hand.

The little body twitched, and Kathy tightened her grip on the knife handle. If she lost her nerve now. . . .

Slowly, she twisted the blade, opening a passage for air, counting the seconds off in her mind, then turning the knife again. There was a sound . . . like a wheezing puff of wind. Without letting up on the slow, rhythmic effort, she called out to Pete.

He had evidently sent the older child into the house, because he came running back alone. "My God, Lynne, what —"

"Lift him up . . . very gently. Wait! Wait'll I tell you this. As you lift him, I've got to keep letting air in and out of his windpipe, so move slowly. When you get him on the seat, I'll manage. Then get us to the hospital — but be careful. No sudden stops."

Pete was too wrung out by now to question her instructions. Between them, they got the child into the old car.

Kathy didn't see what route Pete took. Her eyes didn't leave the little boy's throat. (A quarter turn to the right . . . the pause for inhalation . . . another quarter turn back.)

When they pulled into the emergency driveway at Bayport Community Hospital, the child had partly regained consciousness and was choking on the object in his throat. But he was breathing!

Kathy waited long enough for a crew from Emergency to take charge before dropping her face down on the car seat in a dead faint.

twelve

Kathy opened her eyes to find herself in a strange room. She was lying on a leather couch, and the smell of something like ammonia was heavy in the air.

Turning her head, she saw Petey sitting on the edge of a yellow plastic settee. There were at least a dozen identical matching chairs clustered in groups, each one flanked by a chrome ashtray stand. A television cabinet was in the corner.

Kathy had spent too many coffee breaks in similar surroundings not to recognize a hospital stall lounge. Dizzily, she propped herself up on one elbow, using her "good arm."

Pete jumped out of his seat. "You okay? The nurse said she'd be right back."

"Did you call home?" Kathy asked. Somehow, the first thought that came to her was that Mom Stratton would be worried.

"Sure. Ella's over there. I didn't give Mom any details . . . didn't want to shake her up."

"The little boy?"

"Doin' great — I just got the word. It was the little wheel, all right. I'm still shaking. Me, I'm going into medicine. You're supposed to be squeamish, and yet I still can't figure out how you knew."

"I . . . we had to take a first-aid course in college."

"Oh, sure. Heck, yes. Working around little kids, you'd have to know what to do if. . . ." His forehead gathered in a dubious frown. "They have a nurse around elementary schools, don't they?"

"Not always." Kathy pressed her eyes shut for a moment. "Don't talk about it, Pete. I get faint again just thinking about it."

"I can *imagine*. I wouldn't have had the guts."

A nurse came into the room, beaming at Kathy. "Well! How do you feel?"

"I could . . . use a glass of water."

Pete jumped up, nearly knocking the nurse over in his rush to a water cooler in the corner.

"If you don't feel like a heroine, you should," the nurse said admiringly. She was young and pretty, Kathy noticed. No ring marks on her left hand. One of the "reasonably likable" girls Dane Stratton had apparently overlooked. "Mr. and Mrs.

Rossiter are on their way over. Dane . . . Dr. Stratton's their family doctor, you know."

Pete stumbled over with a paper cup of water filled to the brim, slopping some of it to the floor before Kathy took it from him.

"Thanks, Pete."

"A tracheotomy with my jackknife," he muttered. *"Man!"*

Kathy sipped from the paper cup, sliding over to the edge of the couch and then lowering her feet to the floor. She got up to a sitting position slowly.

"That's the way," the nurse said. "Go easy!" And then she laughed shortly. "Here I am, telling *you*. I guess anybody who can manage *surgery* knows better than to leap up after coming out of a faint." She walked over to the door, looked out into the hall, and came back to the couch. "They're not here yet. But they're going to fall all *over* you, Miss Haley! You saved that boy's life. And, as you may know, Mrs. Rossiter can't have another baby."

"Yeah, that's *right,*" Pete said. "I forgot about that, Claire."

In Bayport, everyone knew you, and there were no secrets! None except mine, Kathy thought miserably.

"I used to work in Surgery, back in Seattle," Claire said. "In Surgery eight hours a *day,* mind you. But I wouldn't have the nerve to do what you did. Gee, are you *sure* you didn't study —"

"Her roommate was a nurse," Pete said. "You know. . . ."

"Oh, yes," she said, dropping her voice in deference to the deceased Kathy Barrett. "I'm sorry I brought it up, Miss Haley."

"Don't worry about it. Pete, I think we ought to be getting home."

"Don't you want to stay until the Rossiters get here? And I know Dane . . . Dr. Stratton wants to see you."

"I'd . . . like to go home now. Please."

The nurse understood, and Petey was more solicitous than ever. After all, what "Lynne" had done would have been a shattering experience, under the circumstances, even for a doctor, or a nurse!

Kathy spent the rest of the day in her bedroom, pleading a headache and extreme nervousness.

Mom Stratton had been spared the more fearsome details, but she had been present when a pair of grateful neighbors came to call on "Miss Haley." She came into Kathy's room afterward, kissing Kathy's cheek and saying, "I told them you're too shaken up to see anyone now, dear. But it's all over town . . . and you can't imagine how Brad and Noreen feel. We all had a good cry, naturally. People keep calling. And if Dane wasn't a doctor, I told Ella, I'd take the phone off the hook."

"It's too much excitement for you, Mom."

"No, no . . . I'm only hearing the nice part. Bobby's fine and you saved him. I wouldn't *let* anyone tell me what actually happened. But when I *think* that you're the same as I am when it comes to those things, I can't believe it!"

"We . . . manage to overcome our fear in an emergency."

"Thank God for that! Lynne, you're nervous as a cat. I'm going to phone Dane and have him come home and give you a sedative."

"No!"

"You see! You're all unstrung!"

"Don't disturb him — please. All I need is rest."

Mom Stratton left her alone after that. But shortly after Kathy had asked to be excused from dinner, Dane knocked on her door and asked, "May I come in, Lynne?"

Intuitively, she had felt that he would

weigh the facts, look into her eyes — and know that she was not the "squeamish schoolteacher" Jim had described in his last letter home. It was difficult to control her nerves when he came into the room.

"Mom tells me you need something to calm you down," he said. He extended his hand, letting it linger for an instant on hers after he had dropped two white tablets into Kathy's palm. He had brought a glass of water with him, and Kathy washed the pills down dutifully, avoiding his eyes.

"Thanks, Doctor."

"Don't thank me. Wait'll you see my bill."

If he was suspicious, he was covering up in an exceptionally congenial manner.

Dane pulled a chair closer to the bed and sat down. "Lynne?"

She continued to stare at the bedspread. "Hm?"

"Do you know how many people out of a hundred know what a tracheotomy is? Barring medical people, that is?"

"Oh . . . I don't know."

"I'd guess maybe ten. And of those, how many do you think would know how it's performed? And when?"

"I haven't any idea." Her voice had risen, edgy and high-pitched now. "I don't want to think about it."

"And out of that percentage," Dane went on in that slow, persistent fashion so typical of him, "would you care to guess how many would be able to do what you did today — and do it as well? I'll tell you; you could count them on one finger."

In the next breath he would tell her that she had lied when he had offered to show her around the hospital, lied when she had told him she was interested in his work but that she "wouldn't be able to take it." His mother had told him, then, that some people were able to separate themselves from pain and bloodshed, while others couldn't; Lynne fell into the latter category, and would he please realize that once and for all?

Kathy waited for the accusing sentence: *You're a nurse! You've seen that operation performed dozens of times! You wouldn't have dared attempt it otherwise! You aren't Lynne Haley — she would have frozen in terror and stood by helplessly while the boy choked to death.*

"You could count them on one finger," Dane repeated. "So, knowing how scared you must have been, I can't tell you how much I respect you." With an admiration that seemed to equal her own for him, he added, "Don't deceive yourself, Lynne.

You would have made a great nurse."

A damned-up wall of tears broke free inside her, and Kathy buried her head in the pillow.

"Lynne, don't cry! Please, don't!" His hand caressed her shoulder — an awkward male touch; the man, not the doctor, bewildered and helpless in the presence of a woman shaken by sobs.

"I know what you've been through . . . this must have been a horrible experience for you. But, Lynne . . . listen to me! Honey, listen . . . please!"

Gently, conscious of the injured arm, he turned her toward him, brushing the tears from her face with his fingertips. "There's nothing to cry about now!"

"Dane, you don't know . . . you don't know."

"I know you're the most wonderful thing that ever happened to us." He was stroking her face now, looking at her with a burning intensity, yet an expression so poignantly tender that Kathy lost hope of controlling the blistering tears. "Lynne . . . that's not all I want to say. You're the most wonderful thing that ever happened to *me*. That's what I want you to know. Maybe this isn't the time . . . I haven't any right. . . ."

Kathy shook her head from side to side. "Don't! Don't say that, Dane. You don't *know* . . ."

He leaned over to plant a brotherly kiss on her forehead. "This isn't doing you any good. I never did have much of a bedside manner." He was hurrying — obviously sorry for what he had said and not waiting to hear what she had to tell him! "Those pills should have you calm and asleep in a few minutes. Good night, Lynne. Everything's . . . fine now."

Kathy pressed her face against her pillow, knowing that sometimes Mom Stratton's prescription for heartache didn't help. Not even a "good cry" was going to make her feel better.

They postponed the excursion to the lake. Kathy's Sunday was spent listening to the praise of friends and neighbors, and in accepting, for one full hour, the thanks of Bobby Rossiter's parents.

From the Rossiters, Kathy learned that Dane had been "Bobby's first friend in the world"; he had delivered the baby less than two years ago.

"And I sometimes think Doctor Stratton loves Bobby as much as we do," Mrs. Rossiter said fondly. It explained Dane's reaction the night before. He had been, like the boy's parents, overwhelmed with gratitude. At breakfast he had been friendly, but impersonal. And he had used the right compliment the first time: "Lynne" was the most wonderful thing that had ever happened, not to *him,* but to the Stratton family.

Among the Sunday visitors was Mrs. Borowski, who came accompanied by a young, auburn-haired companion — another nurse from the hospital. This time Kathy was given a full introduction to the girl she had met in the staff lounge: Claire Ballenger.

Claire was gracious and pleasant, but from the way she looked at Dane, there was little doubt in Kathy's mind that she had maneuvered her presence at Mrs. Borowski's visit with "dear Angie and her daughter" for important reasons of her own. Kathy couldn't dislike the girl. Nor could she blame her for being attracted to, and probably in love with, Dane. It was Kathy's insurmountable handicap that made her insides churn with resentment. Dane had made it clear that he had "no right" to an interest in a girl who was almost Jim's "widow." In the short span of time that had elapsed since the accident, he would have been completely disillusioned if "Lynne" had disagreed with him. In her role as Lynne Haley, Kathy couldn't hope to compete with the aggressive, uniquely attractive R.N.

And Claire evidently knew from close observation that Dane Stratton was dedicated to his profession. While Mrs. Borowski and Mom Stratton chatted over tea at the dining-room table, Claire didn't pointedly exclude Kathy from the living-room conversation, but she held Dane's interest with hospital talk, referring to his currently hospitalized patients, knowingly discussing plans for the new wing, complimenting him on the full recovery of a mutual acquaintance who had been seriously ill.

Dane's contributions were animated and warm; anyone could see that he was in his element and that he enjoyed the medical "shoptalk" immensely. And, tongue-tied, not daring to make comments that crowded her mind, Kathy felt relegated to the position of an outsider, raging with an impotent fury when Dane turned to explain terms that were as familiar to her as the back of her hand.

Pete came in near the tail end of the visit, but he listened long enough to draw an obvious conclusion. While Mom and his brother saw the visitors to the door, he winked at Kathy. "She's really got a case on Dane, hasn't she?" He, too, considered "Jim's girl" out of the running. Certainly the thought that "Lynne" might be jealous didn't cross his mind. "Claire might wake the guy up yet; you can't tell. He probably hasn't noticed that she's a doll, but you know what a soft touch he is for a medical confab. She's got it half made, just being a nurse!"

thirteen

Dane's Tuesday-morning invitation was startlingly unexpected. While Kathy and Ella cleared the breakfast table, he folded up his newspaper, set his pipe down in an ashtray, and said, "This is a day of miracles. I don't have an office appointment before three o'clock. Everybody in the hospital's well enough to be demanding a release, *and*, if any of my mommies come through today, I'll go back to school to learn how to *count!*"

"That's a buildup to going surf fishing," Pete predicted. He was on his way out the door, an armload of books under one arm, a half-eaten banana in the other. "Show her Indian Point, Dane. Man, that's the wildest!"

"What about it, Lynne? I don't want to fish . . . maybe a little beachcombing?"

Pete yelled, "See ya, everybody," and the door banged behind him.

Kathy looked to Mom for an answer. "It sounds great, but I don't like to leave. . . ."

"Ella's going to be here all day," Mom said. "And some of the ladies from church are coming by this morning. Don't stay home on my account, dear. Go on out . . . it'll do you good."

Kathy raced upstairs to change into new jeans and an old bulky sweater, the latter a warm if somewhat shapeless gray item that had belonged to Petey. Mom had urged it upon her because "Lynne" didn't own any "sensible" cold-weather clothes.

Surveying herself quickly in the mirror, Kathy decided the casual effect would please Dane. He wasn't impressed by glamorous trappings. Maybe he would have liked her better in a white uniform, but he *had* asked her to go beachcombing with him. And on Sunday, Claire Ballenger had pointedly mentioned that she would be working the afternoon shift this week, that her mornings would be free — and wasn't Indian Point lovely at this time of the year?

On a high rocky bluff jutting out over a pebbled beach, a grotesquely beautiful cluster of cypress trees bent their gnarled limbs in memory of bygone winds. An opaque white mist drifted over the cliff, but near the water the air was clear. Once in a while the sun broke through to throw a pale yellow light through a low-hanging cloud mass. More often it was obscured, the ocean reflecting the somber gray pall of the sky.

"It's beautiful," Kathy said.

Dane nodded. "I hoped you wouldn't say 'it must be beautiful when the weather's nice.' I like the ocean in all its moods. Most people can't appreciate it unless the sun is bright and the water's blue."

"Oh, no. No, this is dramatic."

"A little ominous."

"Yes, but there's a . . . kind of breathless mystery about it."

Dane was pleased with her reaction. As he guided her down a gradual, shale-covered decline, he held her forearm in a strong grip, and spoke in a voice even more subdued than usual. "When you come here alone in the winter, this quiet, awesome atmosphere gets inside you. I get the same sensation in the delivery room once in a while. It's a little frightening because no matter how much you think you know about life and death, it's still beyond your comprehension. Do you know the feeling, Lynne? Some people find it in a cathedral; some are overcome by it when they listen to music. I get it when a baby's born . . . or out here, on the beach. But not when the sun's out."

"No," Kathy said. "When it's exactly like this. And when you're alone."

"Or with somebody who . . . knows what you're talking about when you describe the feeling."

They reached level ground, crunching through pebbles toward the coarser sand near the water's edge.

"Tide's way out," Dane said. "Good time for finding treasure."

Kathy smiled. "Spanish doubloons?"

"No. A shell . . . or a perfect sand dollar. Maybe a promising piece of driftwood. Pete's been talking about making driftwood lamps for years. Did you see the stack of stuff he has in the garage? Some beautiful pieces, too. So far, it's all talk and no lamps."

"Do you come here often?"

"We used to when we were younger. Jim and Petey and I. Is this going to depress you?" Dane frowned. "I don't know why I didn't think of it. Jim and your friend were killed in a spot just like this . . . just four miles down the line."

Kathy exhaled deeply. Why was everything spoiled with a reminder that she was living a lie? And wasn't the deceit tormenting in itself? When the lies involved Jim, they bordered on sacrilege.

Dane interpreted her silence as a cue to drop the subject. "I haven't had time to come here much in the past few years," he said.

"But you've been here."

"Once in a while."

"Alone?"

"Yes."

"What did you think about, Dane?"

"Walking along like this?"

"Uh-huh."

"Oh . . . I don't know. No, I take it back. One of the things I thought about, quite often as a matter of fact, was being here with someone else."

"Someone special?"

"Special? Yes. But no one in *particular*." Dane stopped to pick up a cluster of purple barnacles, examine the bud-shaped segments, dropping it to the sand again. "Decisions, decisions! They assume great importance down here. Whether or not a shell is worth keeping becomes a major issue."

They walked quietly for a time, Dane concentrating on his search for "treasures," Kathy watching the surprisingly gentle surf. At high tide it would pound beyond the giant rock formations far up on the beach. Now, like everything strong and substantial that she desired, the rocks were within sight, but out of reach.

Dane had a habit of picking up the broken threads of a conversation. "I never visualized my 'special somebody.' Not physically. I conceived a . . . nebulous personality. Someone I could communicate with, whether or not either of us spoke. But, you know . . . if I *had* pictured someone, I think she might have had pale blonde hair that had gotten all tangled from . . . wet salt air. And she probably — no, I'm sure of it — *she'd have worn blue jeans and a beat-up hand-me-down sweater.*"

Kathy slowed her walk, his words touching, exciting, and at the same time unbearably painful. If he didn't return her love, he was hinting a promise that he someday might. And her own love for him had grown too great, too important, in her life to permit Dane's affection for her to be built on sand. Yet she lacked the courage to tell him the truth. Oh, she might begin now to tell him she was a fraud. But she wouldn't finish the first sentence. "Dane. . . ."

He had stopped beside her, looking into her face with that peculiar tenderness she had seen written there once before.

Kathy's voice broke as she cried out his name a second time. "Dane . . . I wish . . . oh, I wish —"

Kathy would have sworn that neither she nor Dane had moved — yet she was in his arms, pressed firmly against his body, the salty-sweet pressure of his lips on hers at once hungry and tender, as though he loved her in all the ways there are to love. And because she had waited so long for love and for this warm, safe, enclosed sense of belonging, Kathy knew that she had not cheated the others as cruelly as she had cheated herself. For you loved this completely only once. And if by some miracle you were loved in return, an embrace such as this should be filled with pure joy. It shouldn't be shoddy or fearful. She should be clinging to Dane ecstatically now, because they had found each other — not holding him tightly because it might be the last time, because tomorrow, the next day, at any moment, the lies would come crushing down over her head and she would lose him completely.

Kathy released herself from his arms reluctantly. "Don't . . . please don't."

Her words had hurt him, but his tone was self-accusing. "I'm sorry, Lynne. I couldn't help myself. I keep forgetting. . . ."

She wanted to scream at him then . . . scream to the world that she had never loved Jim Stratton, never promised to marry him, that she mourned him as a dear friend, but not as the heartbroken woman he would have married if a violent death hadn't separated them. *I'm free to love you,* she wanted to cry. *I'm Kathy Barrett; I'm not too sacred to touch — I was never "Jim's girl" and I'm not crying because he's gone, I'm crying because I love you, Dane . . . I love you!*

She wanted to say all these things, and more, but Dane was walking her back toward the pathway that curved up the side of the bluff; castigating himself for "opening an unhealed wound," for taking advantage of "Lynne's confused emotional state." And promising not to forget, again, that she couldn't free herself of the memory of his brother's love . . . not this soon . . . not this way.

Dane was saying all the wrong things, and he was half agreeing with her when she told him she had to go away.

"I don't want you to go, Lynne. But I can't love you the way I do and have you this close to me. I couldn't promise to stay away from you. And I know you want me to. You're being polite and considerate, but you're not ready to welcome a . . . new love."

On the way home they were solemn, talking about the next "practical" step; "Lynne" would move out of the house soon. She would try to live nearby, stay in touch with the family, visit Mom often. But not while Dane was around. Because, if he couldn't have her, he said, it would be better if he didn't see her at all.

It was the solution Kathy had thought she wanted; an excuse to escape the trap with Dane's blessing. And she had wanted the excuse desperately. Until now, when the thought of separation from Dane Stratton resembled nothing so much as death within life. Ironic justice, she thought bitterly — because somewhere on the outskirts of Bayport a small headstone marked the final resting place of Kathy Barrett.

Mom was talking to one of her old friends in the kitchen when Dane and Kathy returned to the house, but she called out, "You're back early. Was it cold at the point?"

"A little chilly," Dane called back. It was a strained reply; he hated deception, and even this trivial lie was painful to him.

"Mail's on the dining-room table," Mom called.

"Okay; thanks."

Dane was at the foot of the stairway. He was going to bathe and change clothes and go to his office, he told Kathy — even though he had no appointments scheduled for several more hours.

"I may as well look over the bills while the tub's getting filled," he said.

Kathy was close to the dining-room table and she reached over to hand him a large brown envelope and several letters stacked on top of it. And she didn't intentionally look at the return addresses; there was only a swift, unconscious sweep of the eyes . . . and the familiar type she had seen so often on printed forms hurled itself at her: KNOLLSIDE COMMUNITY HOSPITAL.

She was sick with fear, her breath suspended, her insides turning over. *Knowing that this was it . . . this was the time she had dreaded.*

"Thanks," Dane said. He sorted through the white envelopes quickly, holding them in one hand while he looked at the large manila packet. "Something from Larry Forbes," he muttered. "There's a letter from him, too. Might be of interest to you,

Lynne. Let's have a look."

He walked into the living room, Kathy following him, her legs threatening to buckle under her.

They sat down on the sofa and Dane said, "See what's in the big one, I'll read these."

Dane opened the letter from the hospital first, scanning the typewritten page hastily and then saying, "Was your friend in some kind of trouble, Lynne? This is from the administrator . . . he didn't know where to reach you; asked me to let you know that Miss Barrett's been absolved of any responsibility in the —" Dane glanced back at the letter "— the Bailey case. He thought you might be relieved to know her name had been cleared. My God, a homicide? *Euthanasia?* Well, here, you read it later. Let's see what Larry has to say. . . ."

Her hands barely controllable, Kathy ripped the paper tape from the package, while Dane opened the letter from his second cousin in San Francisco.

It was apparently a short note. And perhaps if Kathy had heard Dane read the lines before she pulled the contents out of the accompanying brown envelope, she would have taken them to her room. For after all, they were *intended* for Lynne Haley.

But Dane read the letter aloud too slowly:

"Dear Dane, Under separate cover I am mailing you the last remaining personal effects of Miss Kathy Barrett, which I expect you will want to forward to Miss Haley.

"I presume Miss Haley is no longer at the house and that she would appreciate having these items. They were turned over to me for this purpose by a Mrs. Pick, Miss Barrett's former superior at Knollside Community Hospital. There is nothing of intrinsic value, but a close friend would undoubtedly want the photos, etc., for sentimental reasons. The other contents of Miss Barrett's locker, consisting of a uniform, cap, and two pairs of shoes, I will hold here pending Miss Haley's decision regarding disposal.

"Don't hesitate to phone if there is anything else I can for you here.

"Hope your mother is better. Give her our love and tell her if Martha and I can get away for a weekend soon, we'll drive up to see all of you. Regards to Petey and —"

Dane dropped the letter. His face frozen, his mouth half open, he was staring at an eight-by-ten glossy photograph on Kathy's lap: the topmost picture she had withdrawn from the packet of odds and ends gathered from her hospital locker.

It was a picture taken by a photographer friend of an accident victim Kathy had cared for during her first month at Knollside Community Hospital. She had taped it inside her locker door with white adhesive; the corners had been torn off when it had been removed. But the photo itself was clear and intact: the young gentleman smiling at the world from his wheelchair and, behind the chair, posing with him on the hospital patio, the nurse — the nurse with the black-striped cap that told you that she was an R.N. And the clearly legible inscription written in black ink: "Thanks to Kathy Barrett, the world's best (and prettiest) nurse! Gratefully, Mike O'Sheil."

Mr. O'Sheil's photographer friend had been an expert. Only a blind man could have questioned that the nurse and the girl seated beside Dane Stratton were one and the same.

Kathy was conscious only of the accusing silence, and the complete collapse of her defense. It was over. There wasn't another covering lie inside her; not only because a lie in the face of this evidence would have been futile but also because she was seeing the picture now through

Dane's eyes — experiencing his shock along with her own terror. If the thought had never occurred to him, how quickly would it register now? If someone proved to *her* that Dane Stratton was not Dane Stratton, how long would it take before *she* could absorb the truth?

Kathy said nothing. She closed her eyes, too weak to run or deny or explain. Exposed as a cheat, and vanquished.

Dane studied the picture for a long time. Then, his complexion blanched and every facial muscle rigid, he asked, "Why? Tell me that, Miss Barrett. Why?" His hands shook as he leafed through the other mementoes: several snapshots of Kathy in uniform, posing with other nurses from Knollside; another of Kathy and Lynne, with Kathy in uniform; and another of Lynne Haley and Jim, with their names, the date, and the occasion inscribed on the back: "Lynne and Jim, Fisherman's Wharf, September, 1962."

Dane crammed the souvenir pictures back into the envelope, looking as though he might be sick. His agony and bewilderment were almost palpable. "What did you hope to accomplish? Hadn't we gone through enough — did you have to play games with us?"

"Dane, listen. . . ."

He was on his feet, pacing the living room in long, agitated strides. "Tell me it's one of those crazy misunderstandings people succumb to. Tell me I'm off my rocker, Lynne . . . *Kathy* . . . *Miss Barrett* . . . *Whoever the hell you are and whatever the hell you want from us!*"

"Dane, please . . . I don't want her to hear you!"

He lowered his voice, but the acidity in his tone increased. "Why not? Have you developed a sudden compassion? You weren't squeamish about moving in on a good deal when you knew we were all torn up about Jim and his . . . his *girl!* Couldn't you wait until you were cleared of a . . . murder rap? Did you have to hide out here, *knowing* what you'd do to my mother?"

Kathy gasped for a deep swallow of air. "You know I was confused. You called me *'Lynne.'* You didn't give me a chance to —"

"I didn't give you a chance to tell me you're a liar? At the hospital? Here, in this house? When you did a tracheotomy on a dying kid . . . couldn't you have told me *then?* On the beach, an hour ago, did you have to drag Jim's name in the dust . . . faking a grief you didn't feel . . . letting me hate myself for wanting you because you're. . . ." Dane's voice cracked and it was frightening to see his natural composure shattered, his emotions explosive and close to the surface. Except for her own tears, she might have looked up to see him crying. Dane — the proud, steady, strong, and unshakable Rock of Gibraltar — *crying!*

"Let me explain why I —"

He wouldn't listen. "Didn't you find any opportunities, Miss Barrett? No chances at all to tell us Lynne Haley died with my brother? Or were you too busy laughing up your sleeve? Pulling your act so beautifully that my mother thinks you'rc an angel! Pete worships you. I — damn you — I told you I'm in love with you! Are you satisfied? Is that what you wanted?"

Kathy let the tears roll down her cheeks unchecked. "You won't listen or try to understand, will you?"

"*Understand?* If you'd had any human feeling. . . ."

"You kept telling me how much Mom wanted Lynne to be with her —"

"She wanted *Lynne!* not a —"

"You told me a shock might kill her! And *you* made the mistake, Dane! By the time I knew what was happening, I had to go along . . . or be responsible for hurting her even more than she'd been hurt already!"

"Don't dramatize it, Miss Barrett! It took ingenuity to represent yourself as . . . one of the family. You had to be clever and without a conscience . . . and I'll give you credit. You were! Maybe this was only a dodge for you . . . waiting it out until your trouble at the hospital in Knollside blew over. But you did a magnificent job. You wasted your time as a nurse. You were a good enough actress to make me fall in love with you!"

"Oh, please! Please let me tell you how I tried! I wanted to tell you . . . I hadn't done anything wrong, Dane! At first it was a mistake and I was dazed and . . . sick. You know that! Maybe you don't know what Lynne meant to me. She was the only family I ever had! And Jim . . . we were friends . . . he told everyone at the hospital that I didn't kill that man. Jim had a *heart!* And when he was gone, and Lynne was gone . . . don't you see? *I didn't have anyone!* You've lived in this house all your life, surrounded by people who love you! You can't comprehend it, can you? I lost everyone who cared! I didn't have *anyone!* I don't have anyone now . . . except . . . Mom! . . . and Petey! . . . and you!"

Dane's back had been turned toward

her. He had been facing the fireplace, too consumed by either contempt or anger or confusion, to look at Kathy. And possibly he hadn't listened to what she had tried to tell him; he was probably seething with preconceived prejudices of his own. But when she leaped up, rushing blindly toward the staircase, Dane reached it before she did. "Wait a minute! We haven't said all there is to say!"

"No, because you won't bend an inch, will you? I'm not excusing what I did! I've gone through hell because of it! But I'm admitting I was wrong. Now will you do whatever you want to do and leave me alone? Call the police . . . go in there and tell *her,* if you want to!" Sobbing, Kathy gestured toward the kitchen. "Just let me get —"

Dane's hands gripped her shoulders. "Get out? Get *out,* Miss Barrett? You go! Go ahead; run out of here! Let her know you've made fools of us . . . did everything but dance on Jim's grave! You go! But I'll hold you *responsible* for what happens to her!"

"Dane, don't shout! She'll *hear* you!"

Her warning silenced him abruptly. Dane stood motionless, listening, until animated voices from the kitchen assured him that the angry quarrel hadn't been overheard. Then, in the controlled tone more typical of him, he said, "I'm going to give you the benefit of the doubt. You're an unprincipled cheat, but you're not inhuman. You don't want Mom to know. . . ."

"Not this way, Dane! Let me go away . . . write to her! Let me do what I told you about at the beach: fade out of the picture gradually. Then you can think whatever you like about me."

Dane hadn't released his angry hold on her shoulders. His fingers tightened now, pressing into Kathy's flesh. "You don't want to hurt her. . . ."

"You know that, Dane! Oh, please . . . you've got to know that!"

"Then you aren't going to leave. You aren't going to clear your conscience at her expense! When I think she's strong enough, and when we can ease you out of the picture without upsetting her, you can go. But not this suddenly, Miss Barrett. Not now! Not until I tell you it's time."

Kathy covered her face with her hands. She was whispering now, conscious of the old woman in the kitchen. (*Mom!* Dane couldn't take that from her . . . she loved his mother; she had earned the right to call her Mom!) "I won't shock her. I'll try to get out soon, but I won't shock her. Let me go, Dane. I want to go upstairs."

He let her go, releasing the restraining grip and turning away from her. "Take the rest of your souvenirs with you." Dane thumbed toward the sofa. "I don't want anyone else disillusioned."

Burning with shame, Kathy crossed the room to pick up the brown envelope. "I wish we could talk. I wish there was a way to. . . ."

Dane wasn't listening. He was on his way up the stairs, leaving everything unsettled and uncertain — all except the fact that Kathy Barrett had deceived him, and that she wasn't going to run from the misery she had caused. He would tell her when to go, but for the time being, he expected her to go on living her lie.

fourteen

"How come Dane didn't get here for dinner?" Pete asked. "This morning he said business was slack."

Mom Stratton frowned her disapproval. "Peter! You know how Dane feels about that phrase!"

"Can't a guy wisecrack at his own dinner table? What I meant was, he's not in his office and he's not at the hospital. I tried to call him, to see if he wants to go to the game tonight."

"All I know is that he phoned and told me he wouldn't be home for dinner," Mom said. "That's not unusual, is it?"

Pete finished his dessert. "I guess not. But, man, he's sure out on a couple of long house calls."

"You shouldn't worry Mom," Kathy said. She had been silent through most of the meal, and the comment emerged lifeless and barely audible.

"He knows I don't worry about Dane. I've lived with his erratic schedule too long to get upset if he misses a meal." Mom turned to Kathy. "I'm worried about *you*, dear. You don't look a bit well."

"I'm . . . fine."

"You're pale and you've barely said a word since you got back from the beach."

"Don't argue with Mom," Pete grinned. "She's the infallible diagnostician." He gulped down the last of his milk, gathered up the fruit dishes, and dropped several pieces of silverware before he transported the stack to the kitchen. From the sink, he yelled, "Don't forget — *that* woman is a doctor's *mother*. If she tells you you're feeling lousy, you're feeling *lousy*. Even if you feel great!"

Mom shook her head and sighed, but she smiled immediately afterward as Pete returned to the dining room.

"Wish I could ask you to come along, Lynne," Pete said. "This isn't a league game, we have those on Friday nights. This is a big traditional grudge thing. See . . . every year Chatsville clobbers us in football. Then we come back and pin their ears back playing basketball. It's been going on for fourteen years, just like that."

"I'd get Ella to come and stay," Mom said. "But I don't think Lynne's in the mood for a lot of screeching teenagers."

"Teenagers? Listen, all the alumni comes

to this game — and that's half the town. Last year Dane was hoarse for a week afterward. Hey, you sure you don't want me to get Ella? I could swing around and pick her up while you get ready."

"I don't think so, Petey. Thanks."

"You don't know what you're missing. Man, there's so many kids coming from Chatsville, the school board had to rent extra bleachers. What a hassle!"

"Will you be playing?" Kathy asked listlessly. She had to express some kind of interest; Mom was beginning to wonder if something had gone wrong this morning.

"Nab. I'm third string. The coach might use me in a league game. All I can do there is lose him a trophy. If he put Fumble-foot Stratton in against Chatsville, he might get lynched by the alumni." Pete leaned down to kiss his mother's temple. "No wild parties while I'm gone, Angie. See that she lays off the booze, Lynne."

Mom gave him a playful shove. "Oh . . . *you!*"

Pete laughed and hurried toward the door. "I gotta get over to Harriet's house . . . we're making signs to carry. Y'know . . . 'Bruins, Si! Chargers, No!' And, 'Next Time, Chatsville, Don't Take the Bus — Stay Home and Leave Basketball to Us!'

We've got better ideas, too. Hey . . . I'll see you!" Pete pulled the door open. "When Dane gets here, tell him I couldn't wait!"

After the door slammed behind him, the silence was oppressive. Kathy got up to finish clearing the table, conscious of the strained atmosphere, wondering if it were only a projection of her own uneasiness.

Dane had said one last thing to her before he left the house. She was to pretend that nothing had changed. *Pretend* — after that soul-shattering exposure? Maintain the pleasant status quo, with every miserable atom of her body threatening to explode?

Because something had to be said, she mentioned Petey's excitement. "I'm glad you're so patient, Mom. He's noisy, but . . . it's good to see him enthusiastic, isn't it?"

"Yes. He was spending a lot of time in his room, looking depressed." Mom pushed her chair back. "I knew he'd bounce back, though. Jim was the same way."

"Don't get up. I can get these few dishes."

Mom insisted upon helping. In the kitchen, she seemed to avoid mention of Dane, or his absence, though she certainly knew that he wouldn't normally spend from one until seven p.m. on house calls, without being in touch with his office. Had she overheard the argument? Did she suspect . . . or know?

Kathy concluded that she didn't. Everything was peaceful and unchanged in Mom Stratton's little sphere, and Dane expected it to remain that way. At a price, Kathy thought — "a price I can't pay. He may avoid me, but he can't stay out of my way completely. And when he looks at me with contempt in his eyes, I won't be able to pretend any more! I can't do it *now!*"

Kathy escaped to her room by agreeing that perhaps she didn't feel as well as she might. Mom stayed downstairs to write a letter to Larry Forbes and his wife, encouraging their promised visit; Dane had told her about *that* part of the attorney's letter, but nothing more.

Behind her closed bedroom door, Kathy could hear the radio downstairs; an organ concert played nightly over the local station by one of Angie Stratton's innumerable friends. The solemn music was uplifting to Mom; she found spiritual solace in the rich, heavy chords. Kathy found that the music only accentuated her depression.

For a time, she considered packing her belongings, explaining to Mom that she needed a change, and getting out of the house before Pete and Dane returned. Kathy opened her empty suitcases on the bed and got as far as the drawer in which she had hidden Lynne's personal papers, and her own. Tears splashed over Lynne's college annual, and Kathy returned it to its place, throwing herself across the bed beside the open suitcases and sobbing her misery.

Dane would change his mind. He couldn't hope to hold her to the unbelievable bargain. It seemed incredible now that Kathy had made it herself; Dane was too honest to be a conscious party to her deceit. And how long could either of them hope to avert a second exposure — one that might not escape Mom Stratton's notice — a crushing, possibly *fatal,* exposure? No, Dane would listen to reason. He might despise her and she might never see him again, but he would let her go. Tomorrow, after easing the way with a long conversation with Mom, Kathy could pack and leave without shocking Dane's mother.

When she had exhausted her tears, Kathy gave thought to the next move. Again the inevitable questions: Go where?

Do what? She couldn't continue the lie elsewhere, it was unthinkable. Nowhere but in this house was there any justification for the masquerade.

What would be the charge for making a clean breast of it to the authorities? And if she did that, wouldn't her record be damaged forever, so that even if she became Kathy Barrett, R.N., once more, no hospital would hire her? Forgery — she had falsified Lynne's signature. After a jail sentence, where could she apply for a nursing position?

No matter *what* happened, wouldn't the truth eventually get back to Mom? Kathy's fingers raked across her face; it was like living and reliving a nightmare, over and over, always returning to the point at which you had begun. An hour, maybe two, went by. She was no closer to a solution than when she had closed herself in the room.

And perhaps the sharpest of all the needle points jabbing at her was the realization that once she left this house, where she had been loved, she could never return. She had been given a brief taste of what it meant to belong, which would serve only to deepen her sense of loss when it was over. Tonight, referring to the basketball game, Petey had said, "You don't know what you're missing." Until her acceptance in the Stratton home, Kathy had wished and visualized, but she had not truly known what she was missing.

I'll know now, she thought miserably. Mom, Pete, Dane — each of the loves they had offered to her was different from the other, her love for each of them unique. *I'll know now — I'll know for the rest of my life.*

Downstairs, the hour-long organ concert had been concluded. A Strauss waltz floated up the stairway. Kathy got up from her bed, splashed water on her face in the adjoining bathroom, and decided to join Mom Stratton. It wasn't fair to leave her alone, especially with Mom thinking that "Lynne" was ill and depressed.

As she came down the stairway, Kathy heard the lilting melody end, as if Mom had tired of it and flicked the dial. She was almost at the foot of the stairs before the announcer's voice came on, tense and penetrating:

> Ladies and gentlemen, we interrupt our program of Fireside Favorites to bring you an emergency news bulletin. A report has reached this studio that a temporary bleacher set up for tonight's

basketball game in the Bayport High School gymnasium has collapsed. First reports give no details regarding injuries. Please stand by. . . .

There was a deadly pause, during which Kathy looked around anxiously for Mom. Maybe she hadn't heard. She may have left the radio on and gone to her room.

"Lynne! Did you hear?"

Kathy's head spun in the direction of that agonized voice.

"Petey's there! Petey and hundreds of boys and girls! All our friends!"

Mom was seated at the dining-room table, her eyes wide with alarm. A neat stack of addressed envelopes rested in front of her, and she had evidently been writing another letter.

"Take it easy, Mom! The announcer didn't say anyone was hurt." Kathy put her arm around the older woman, steadying her. The Strauss waltz resumed where it had been cut off.

"Whatever you do, stay calm. It's probably a minor accident . . . kids whooping it up a little and maybe —"

"I've been writing letters to all the people out of town." Her voice trembled, and Kathy feared that Mom's panic might precipitate an attack. "Just finishing up . . . thanking them for . . . consoling me about Jim. . . ."

Kathy pressed the trembling shoulder under her hand reassuringly. "I'm sure everything's going to be —"

The recorded waltz was cut off once more. There was a staticlike crackle, and then the announcer's voice again, more agitated this time:

> "We interrupt our program to bring you another report from Bayport High School, where an overcrowded temporary grandstand has collapsed. Rescue units from the police and fire stations have been dispatched to the scene, and two ambulances from Bayport Community Hospital are reported to have arrived at the school. An eyewitness reports that panic and hysteria followed the splintering crash that sent — one moment please!"

Mom's face had been drained of its color. Kathy's mind searched for a calming word, but there was nothing plausible to say, nothing that would reduce the suspense. The local announcer was someone Mom knew. His son attended school with

Pete; he wouldn't dramatize a trivial situation with that tremulous quality in his voice. He was genuinely alarmed.

And again the announcer: "One moment please!"

"I'm frightened, Lynne!"

"Everything's going to be all right. You'll see!"

"But he said . . . *ambulances*."

It wouldn't help to assure Mom that nothing bad had happened at the gym — not when the next report would contradict that assurance. A screaming siren could be heard now from the direction of Oceanside Avenue. Outside the house, a car horn honked impatiently; other people had undoubtedly heard the news and were headed for the school, which was only nine blocks away.

The announcer repeated *"Please stand by!"* several times. Then he came back on the air with an official bulletin from the Bayport Police Department. Congested streets and relatives attempting to crowd into the high school were preventing quick evacuation of the more seriously injured victims.

Mom gasped, and Kathy's grip tightened on her arm. "Easy!"

Police Chief Robert S. Tanner has issued a warning to the effect that all nonmedical persons are to stay clear of the area. Repeat: If you are not associated with the police or fire department, and if you are not a qualified doctor or nurse, do not obstruct the traffic in the block bound by Avenues G and F, Castellano Drive, and Cypress Street. All persons entering the area not in these categories will be arrested!

The announcer's formal appeal was dropped suddenly and was replaced by a more personal, ad-libbed plea to the local citizenry:

Folks, please don't attempt to go to the high school! There are a number of seriously injured youngsters who can't be rushed to the hospital if you block the streets. Names of the injured will be broadcast as soon as we receive them. There are no known dead. However, all available medical personnel are asked to report to Bayport Community Hospital or to the scene of the accident, whichever is closest to you. Repeat: If you are a qualified doctor or nurse, and within range of my voice, please report to the hospital or to the high school. All others, please stay away from the area. Please stand by for additional bulletins.

Someone at the radio station had replaced the gay waltz with a symphonic record more in keeping with the news. Mom Stratton closed her eyes for a moment. When she opened them, there was a new strength and determination in her voice. "You should go, dear. I know you *want* to."

Want to? How could she know how desperately the call of duty tugged at Kathy? "I'm not . . . really qualified," Kathy said. "But if they need help. . . ."

"Petey may be hurt. If not Petey, there are still all those others. You wouldn't be arrested, dear. Everyone in town knows what you did for Bobby Rossiter."

Kathy's mind seized at the flimsy excuse. The police wouldn't let her through because she had performed well in one emergency. But if she could convince them by wearing the little pin buried in the bottom of the drawer upstairs. . . .

"I'll be all right — go ahead!"

"I can't leave you alone, Mom! Not when —" Kathy couldn't finish the sentence. But Mom wasn't so stunned that she couldn't finish it for herself. If she heard that something had happened to her youngest son, the already overly shocked heart might stop beating.

"I'm going to walk over to the telephone," Mom said with exaggerated calm and precision. "I'm going to phone Ella, and if she can't come over, I'll go next door to the Silsbeys. You're not to worry about me. You're to go where people need you. *Young* people!"

She got up from her chair slowly and carefully, as though she were determined to take care of herself, because she couldn't bear to add to the chaos with a cardiac attack. As though she didn't dare influence Kathy's decision by a show of weakness!

Kathy hesitated. "If you're sure . . . I could wait until Ella gets here and —"

"Let me call the Silsbeys. They'll be over in two minutes, you know that." And as if she had read the question ringing in Kathy's mind, Mom said, "This is what Dane would want you to do. It's the *right* thing to do. Now hurry!"

"Mom . . . if anything happened to you." Kathy's eyes filled with tears — tears of admiration for the old woman's courage. Mom was going to wait beside the radio, and for news that might destroy her.

"Nothing's going to happen to me,"

Mom said. "Go where you're needed." She drew a long, deep breath that was like a prayer. "I'll be here waiting for you when you get back — Kathy."

It took a moment before the name registered. But the love and gentleness with which the two revealing syllables had been pronounced erased doubts and fears. "Mom . . . you know! You know I'm —"

"I know you'd better get to the school! Pete walked over to Harriet's . . . his car's in the driveway. Key's on the mantle."

Kathy took time to hug her. "Pete's all right. Keep thinking that. I'll send him home to you. I promise!"

"I believe you, dear," Mom said. "You keep remembering that. Now hurry!"

fifteen

Kathy turned the jalopy into Cypress Street, slowing down as a policeman on foot waved a flashlight and signaled her to the curb.

An ambulance wailed by, and the officer ran to where Kathy had braked Pete's old car to a stop. "You can't get through, lady. You'd better go back home . . . I'll have to arrest you if you go any farther."

"I'm a nurse," Kathy told him. She had never said the three words with greater pride.

"You sure? If you've got somebody at the school . . . most of the kids have been channeled out to the parking lot . . . we're keeping two lanes open on the next street, but we've got to have —"

"I'm sure!" Kathy cried impatiently. "If I can't drive any closer, I'll walk."

The officer looked at the tiny pin Kathy had taken time to affix to her sweater. "Okay, go ahead. You can't drive, though. And from what I saw inside there, you better run."

Kathy ran, covering the block-long distance breathlessly. Police cars and a standby fire engine blocked the street on her left. There were almost no pedestrians or gawkers. A boy in royal blue satin shorts and an athletic shirt labeled Chatsville Chargers came out of the building, one arm supporting a pretty girl of about sixteen. She looked dazed, and a white bandage around her forehead indicated that she had been given first aid. "We'll find your sister," the boy was saying. "I'll bet she's out here somewhere."

The girl only shook her head. "She's still back there! Under all those boards."

Kathy accelerated her steps. At the gymnasium door, another policeman asked for her identification, moving aside quickly at her mention of two respected letters: R.N.

"They're getting everything organized now . . . ten minutes ago everybody was running and yelling. Listen, you're supposed to report over there in the corner. There's a Red Cross lady there."

Kathy raced across the wide wooden floor. On one side of the high-ceilinged building, a corps of men and women worked feverishly over a number of figures — some lying prone, others seated among the debris of gray boards and collapsed metal tubing. Here and there someone called for more gauze or for a doctor's advice, the words echoing in the cavernous, brightly lit room. Men, working quickly but cautiously, were busy moving parts of the wreckage. There was no unnecessary conversation.

Pete Stratton was nowhere to be seen. But near a corner of the room, where a long table had been pressed into service as a medical-supply center, Kathy nearly stumbled over a smashed sign. Its carrying stick had been splintered, and there were footprints and traces of blood on the white window shade on which amateurish letters had been painted. Kathy, swallowing hard, read the message: "Next Time, Chatsville, Don't Take the Bus — Stay Home and Leave Basketball to Us!"

There wasn't time to worry about Pete; she could only hope that he had gone home or to the hospital for minor treatment.

People raced back and forth from the collapsed bleachers to the table; apparently the woman in the red-flowered house-dress was in charge. She had her back to Kathy, handing first-aid supplies to another woman not in uniform; probably an off-duty nurse who had responded to the summons. When the nurse rushed back to the bleacher area, Kathy said, "Can you use me? I'm an R.N."

"Can we use you! Honey, we —" The woman in the print dress turned to face Kathy. It was Mrs. Borowski. "Oh, Lynne. Dear, I know you want to help, but the doctor gave orders that —"

"I'm an R.N.," Kathy repeated stubbornly. "Look . . . here's my pin!"

"But I *know* better, Lynne! I'm sorry, but you're taking up valuable time." Mrs. Borowski started to open a carton of two-inch-wide bandage rolls. "We're very busy!"

"Mrs. Borowski, I want to be put to work!"

"Put her to work," a deep, toneless voice said.

Mrs. Borowski and Kathy turned at the same time. Dane looked tired and disheveled, but he was quite obviously in charge. "She's a nurse," he told Mrs. Borowski. Ignoring her reaction, he told Kathy, "I have a kid over there with severe head and shoulder lacerations and possible rib fractures. Get to him first. Mrs. B., she'll need a kit. And then get someone to call the hospital. Tell them I'm on my way over. I can do more on the other end now."

Dane crossed the gym with Kathy, obviously grim and in a hurry, yet completely self-possessed. "Mom hear the news?"

"She's all right. But I haven't seen Pete."

"I haven't either."

A board clattered to the floor, making loud, repeated, hollow sounds like shots fired in a cave. There was still the possibility of finding someone under that pile of lumber; neither Dane nor Kathy mentioned the fact.

"How bad is it?"

"I've sent at least two criticals out of here. A number were serious, but it could have been worse." He led her to a boy about Pete's age, and Kathy knelt down beside the stretched-out, barely conscious form. "He's had morphine. He's to go in the next ambulance. You know what to do."

Kathy nodded. A gash above the boy's left eyebrow demanded her attention. She was busy attending to the wound when Dane hurried out of the building.

By ten o'clock, the last accident victim had been cleared from the gymnasium — and the last section of the wrecked bleachers removed. Apparently no one had been under the flimsily assembled tiers when they collapsed under the weight of too many wildly excited, stomping kids. Kathy, relieved, drew a deep breath. The building was deserted now, except for a handful of officers, insurance officials, and some nurses.

"Coming to the hospital?" Mrs. Borowski asked Kathy.

Kathy ran a hand over her forehead. It had been weeks since she had tended to patients, and she had never performed under these hectic emergency conditions. Not in volume. Not twenty or thirty frightened, bruised, bleeding, and stunned youngsters; she had lost count, hurrying from one to the next, making forced, on-the-spot decisions when an ambulance attendant asked, "Who goes next?"

"Lynne." Mrs. Borowski repeated. "I asked if you're coming to the hospital."

"Oh. Oh, yes. Yes, if they want me."

"They'll be shorthanded. We always are, but tonight it must be a madhouse. Those poor kids . . . and no one here but Doctor Stratton at first. It was horrible. . . ." Mrs. Borowski ran her thoughts together in weary, disconnected patterns. "Do you have a car here?"

"Yes."

"A neighbor brought me over as soon as we heard. 'Course, I'm on duty in the morning, but they're going to need all the help they can get tonight."

"I have Pete's car parked on the next block."

"Oh . . . good. I'm too tired to walk all that way."

They stepped out of the gymnasium into the cool, damp night air. "You didn't happen to see Pete, did you, Mrs. Borowski?"

"No-o, I can't recall that I did. Was he . . . oh, I expect he was at the game tonight. He was probably over on the other side of the gym. Went on home, I'll bet. That boy wouldn't let Angie fret one extra minute."

"I'll check at the hospital before I call home," Kathy said.

As they drove toward the hospital, Mrs. Borowski said, "You know, I would have sworn Angie and everyone else said . . . why, you said it *yourself!* That you were a *schoolteacher!*"

Kathy was too disheartened for confessions, explanations, or excuses. And the only people who mattered already knew the truth. "I lied," she said flatly. "I lied and lied."

The elderly head nurse looked puzzled, but she didn't pry beyond that startling admission. She changed the subject, and for the rest of the short trip they discussed the disastrous Chatsville–Bayport "grudge game," which neither side had won.

Minutes after her arrival at the hospital, Kathy was on duty in Emergency Service, wearing a borrowed uniform, oxfords belonging to Claire Ballenger, and one of Mrs. Borowski's caps.

Normally, a patient didn't stay in Emergency long. There was no reconstructive work attempted here; if an injury case required immediate surgery, pain was alleviated, hemorrhage was stopped, the blood type was checked and cross-checked, and saline or whole blood was given to counteract shock.

Tonight, the process was far from normal. Extra cots lined the walls of the corridor outside. The two critical cases had been cared for first; the injuries considered "serious" had been given attention next; by now they were in the custody of Bayport's regular nursing staff on the upper floor.

But the greater part of the injured parties had been typical Emergency Service cases. With only two doctors who could be spared from the life-and-death dramas being played upstairs, the staff R.N.'s and the volunteer nurses jumped to terse commands from exhausted superiors.

Kathy found her mind, body, and emotions submerged in the vital work. This was her purpose — this was her life. She would have preferred to wear the uniform again under other conditions, but these were the circumstances under which she had been called. Kathy utilized her compassion, knowledge, and experience through trained hands and watchful eyes.

Once in a while, though he seemed to be needed more by the critically injured youngsters, Dane would lend his services in the Emergency areas. Kathy would find herself working at his side then, knowing that if she had earned his contempt, after tonight she would also be worthy of his respect. He might despise her, but he would pay her his ultimate compliment: "You're a good nurse."

It was after three a.m. when the last patient had been either dismissed or wheeled upstairs for further treatment and observation. The last frantic parent had been reunited with a missing son or daughter and the last bandage securely fastened. It wasn't until then that Kathy remembered that she had been rushed into service so quickly that she had forgotten to call Mom Stratton.

She found Dane in a dimly lit vestibule just inside the wide doors to which the ambulances had brought their pathetic cargoes all evening. The doors were open and he seemed to be drawing the cold air into his lungs desperately.

"Doctor Stratton?"

He turned to face her, his expression revealing a beaten, animal weariness. "I imagine you need a ride home. You look tired."

"No more than anyone else. What I wanted to tell you was . . . I haven't called your mother since I left the house. I'm worried . . . about her. And about Pete."

"Pete isn't there," Dane said. "And my mother's asleep. I had the switchboard operator call home and I had Ella give her a couple of sleeping tablets."

"Pete's not there?" The frozen breath again . . . the sharp pang of fear! Kathy covered her mouth with her hand, as if to stifle a shocked cry. "What's wrong? He wasn't down here. Dane — *he isn't one of those kids upstairs?"*

Dane studied what must have been stark terror in her eyes. "You care. You really do care!"

"Oh, Dane, it's terrible for any of the

families . . . we know what they're suffering. But Petey! After what you and Mom have had to face!"

"Kathy."

She lowered her eyes. He had said her name softly, without vindictiveness or sarcasm, but coming from him it had an alien sound that flooded her with shame.

"Kathy, could *you* go to sleep tonight not knowing if Pete were safe?"

"You know I couldn't! Please . . . if you could just believe *that* much."

"Then what makes you think Mom could? He phoned her. From somewhere between here and Chatsville. I got the message third hand and in a rush, so I don't know the details."

"But he's not hurt?"

"That's what he told Mom. And she told Ella and Ella told the gal at the switchboard. And I found out the last time I ran past the reception desk. Don't ask me what he was doing way out wherever he was."

"He doesn't even have his car! I drove it to the school."

Dane was leaning against the doorframe now, looking as though he would collapse without the support. "Before you drove it to the school, Kathy, what excuse did you give my mother?"

"I . . . didn't have to give her an excuse."

"I meant . . . she would have known a 'squeamish schoolteacher' wouldn't head for a disaster scene."

"Are you afraid I told her? That I was capable of hurting her, just to get out of my predicament?"

He looked deep in thought for a moment, and then he muttered, "You didn't tell her."

"She told me to go. She . . . called me by my name!"

"Your —"

"I don't know how she found out, but she knew. Somehow, she wasn't shocked. She was calmer and braver than anyone I've ever seen in a grave situation. And she said 'Kathy,' as if she had never called me anything else."

"Don't start to cry, Kathy."

"I won't. I can't any more."

"You're too exhausted."

"No. It's just that there aren't any tears left. I shed too many over . . . what happened back at Knollside. A patient I had barely seen . . . and suddenly I was accused of —"

"That's over," Dane said firmly. "After I left you this . . . when was it, this morning? This afternoon? I phoned the administrator at Knollside. Mrs. Bailey's suffered a complete mental breakdown. But she's . . . lucid enough on one subject. She gave her husband an overdose of barbiturates. You wouldn't have had to cry long, Kathy."

"Maybe not there. But Lynne. You won't ever know how close we were. We weren't raised in your Mom's house, Dane. *We* grew up wearing dingy uniforms and eating oatmeal for breakfast every morning, but that didn't matter. What mattered was . . . no one ever came into that crowded dorm to kiss us good night . . . only to tell us to be quiet."

"I didn't want to remind you —"

"You don't have to remind me! Do you think I've ever forgotten? You can remember your dad. He ran the corner drugstore. You ran errands for him and he fixed you extra-large strawberry sundaes at the soda fountain. Maybe you lost him, but you've got that to remember. I can remember my mother saying only that Frank Barrett was a drunken bum."

She wasn't tearful or angry or contrite. The long night's demands upon her senses had dulled them, so that she was reciting words now like a dull, toneless litany . . . saying them not in the hope that they would be believed or would change the way Dane felt about her, but because they had lain unspoken inside her for so long.

And because Dane was listening, motionless, his eyes never leaving her face.

"I've cried myself out about that, Doctor. And about your brother. Did you think anyone who knew Jim as a friend *wouldn't* cry? I wasn't lying about . . . *everything,* was I? The tears were real. And there were so many . . . so many that, now I'm . . . awfully tired . . . and there . . . aren't any more."

He may have thought from the faintness of her tone that she was going to crumple to the floor. And then again he may only have reached out for her because he wanted her in his arms. Kathy wasn't certain. She let him hold her, neither of them saying any more, closing her eyes tightly and letting the merciful tiredness claim her.

Sometime afterward — it may have been only seconds later — she was vaguely aware that Dane was carrying her into the night, that a car door opened, closed. And then she was lying on a wide, softly upholstered seat, and the quiet hum of a motor was related in some obscure way to going home, where she belonged.

sixteen

Kathy awoke on a couch in the Strattons' living room. She was covered with a blanket, and a pillow had been slipped under her head. It took a few seconds to realize why she had gone to sleep in a borrowed nurse's uniform and where she had gotten the white oxfords resting side by side next to the sofa.

Her watch was still running. It was 8:46. In the *morning?* Sunlight from a slit in the draperies cut a brilliant swath across the floor. She wasn't *sure,* but it sounded as if someone was scraping toast in the kitchen.

Kathy got up from the couch and followed the sound, finding a slightly bedraggled, but unharmed, Pete attempting to rescue a charred slice of bread from disgrace with a knife.

"Pete! If you knew how you worried us! Where'd you *go?*"

He was examining the wrinkled uniform and Kathy's nyloned, shoeless feet. "You should ask! Where've *you* been in that outfit? Man, I walk in, about 8:15, I think it was. Dane's gone, Mom's sound asleep upstairs, and you're out like a light in there." He thumbed toward the living room. "What goes *on?* What's with the *nurse* getup?"

"I worked at the school last night, Pete. And at the hospital."

Pete nodded dumbly. In an emergency, the layman might have to be put to work. "That was rough last night. It still hasn't dawned on me."

"Were you there?"

"Was I there? I'm sitting next to this girl, and all of a sudden she's yelling 'Yea, Chargers!' So I tell her she's on the wrong side of the gym. Well, there's this thing about meeting a girlfriend who goes to Bayport. And how she came with a guy from Chatsville, and he's on the other side of the building, *looking* for her girlfriend. Y'see?"

"I'm not sure, but you seem to be."

"Well, this is a cute chick, and I figure maybe her boyfriend got lost. Anyway, we're kind of kidding back and forth about who's got the sharper team. And she points out this guy. He's coming around the side of the bleachers. Doesn't look like he found this Bayport girl. Anyway, by that time there's not a chance of cramming him into a seat, and everybody's going wild and stamping their feet. See, it was time out in the second quarter, and we're tied, nineteen to nineteen.

"The last I see of this kid, he's swinging up the side of the bleachers. That's not what did it, but that's when we hear this loud crack. And suddenly everybody's falling all over everybody, and screaming, and the whole thing practically flattens out.

"I didn't know what I was doing. So help me, I . . . got up. Had a rough time getting out of the mess, but I knew I wasn't hurt. And there's this girl screaming like crazy. I sort of blanked out for a while, I guess. Then she's back again. Man, it was awful; so many kids hurt, everything all mixed up. Anyway, her boyfriend's the first guy they carried out of there. Hurt bad. I got his name from her, and I heard on the radio at the bus station he's still in bad shape, but he's off the critical list."

"Pete . . . where'd you *go?*"

"I told you, she was all shook up. She was hysterical. Partly because of this kid, and partly . . . well, they came in her dad's car, and she didn't know how to drive, and she was scared because she wasn't supposed to be in Bayport. Her folks had nixed the idea, and the car was borrowed just to go to a drive-in in Chatsville."

"So you drove her home."

"What could I do? She was so scared. . . ."

"And you took the bus back?"

"What else was there? And the buses don't run all night. I had to wait till six o'clock. And all the way home I kept thinking, why didn't I stay there and help the kids that were hurt? Dane's gonna shoot me, but . . . I wasn't *thinking* straight. When something like that happens, you . . . I don't know. You don't always *think* straight! Tell that to Dane, will you? Me, the big, upcoming medic . . . I pull a dumb stunt like that. Run out . . . scare everybody sick. Man, will *Dane* let me have it! Can you say something to him, Lynne?"

She didn't wince at the name, which came so naturally to Pete. "I can try."

"He's a doctor. He ought to know!" Pete set the blackened toast aside and opened the refrigerator. "I'm starved, are you? How 'bout if I fix bacon and eggs?"

"Fine," Kathy said.

Pete hauled out a cardboard egg box, narrowly missing dropping it to the floor. "Man! I give up on the doctor bit. I'm so clumsy . . . I'm the family misfit."

Kathy didn't tell him that she had first claim to the title. Pete was fishing the bacon from out of the meat tray and saying, "Like I said, Dane's a doctor. He shouldn't have to be told that when you come out of a big shock . . . you're liable to do something you're sorry for."

"I hope he knows that," Kathy said softly. "I hope he understands that now, Pete."

Kathy had exchanged the soiled and creased uniform for slacks and a sweater. Minutes after she had returned to the kitchen to clean up Pete's attempt at making breakfast, and seconds after Pete had dragged himself up to his room, Mom Stratton came downstairs.

Kathy met her in the dining room. "Mom? Did you get a good night's rest? Pete's home, you know."

"You told me he would be," Mom said. She looked rested, and she insisted upon hearing all the details of the night before, including the latest broadcast report from the hospital.

"They've taken a boy from Chatsville off the critical list," Kathy told her. "The other critically injured person is the school custodian. Last word is that he's holding his own."

"Dane's still at the hospital?"

"I think so. I don't even remember him bringing me home. And he must have gone right back after that."

Mom shook her head disparagingly. "I hope Petey doesn't decide to go into medicine."

Kathy smiled. "I don't think you have to worry." She pulled a chair out from under the big table. "Sit down, Mom. I'll have your orange juice in a second."

"You're tired, dear."

"No, I'm not. I . . . never felt better. More like —"

"Like yourself, Kathy?"

"Yes."

In another moment, in spite of what she had told Dane about having touched bottom in her well of tears, she thought she might begin to cry again. It wouldn't be good for Mom. She'd had her full share of emotional scenes.

Kathy walked into the kitchen, keeping her voice as casual and steady as possible. "How did you know, Mom? And how long?"

"From the instant you walked into my room that first morning."

Kathy sliced three oranges in two on the breadboard and turned on the electric squeezer. When the juice glass was full, she carried it into the dining room. "But *how* did you know?"

"A day or two before she left Knollside, Lynne must have had qualms about meeting her . . . prospective mother-in-law. She wrote to me. Didn't think it was right to come 'barging in' unless I knew something about her. She knew the kind of letters Jim wrote. Short and funny, but very few concrete facts."

"Lynne *wrote* to you!"

"Told me all about herself. And enclosed a snapshot. I never showed it to Dane or to Pete. The day her letter arrived, we . . . got the call from the police. After that, I didn't want to add to the misery. And when you came into the room upstairs, Kathy, I knew you weren't Jim's girl. I knew you were as unhappy as I was . . . but I still had two of my boys. You were all alone. In some kind of trouble. I didn't know what . . . but I knew you needed our love. And we'd just . . . lost an important outlet." Mom blotted her eyes with a corner of her print apron. "I could have saved you a lot of misery by saying something that first morning. I was a little selfish, Kathy. I wanted you to stay — I helped you into that terrible trap."

"And then you found yourself having to

lie, right along with me."

"Did either of us know what it would mean? To give up being yourself? Every day the noose seemed to get tighter. I grew more and more afraid of telling Dane. That was our biggest mistake — not trusting Dane."

Mom was assuming half the guilt, talking as though she had been a fellow conspirator. Kathy walked over quickly to hug her. "You should have hated me at sight."

"Hated?"

In that incredulous inflection, Kathy recognized Mom Stratton's entire simple philosophy. "That's a foreign word to you, isn't it, Mom?"

Mom sipped her orange juice. "I've spent a lifetime trying to make it a foreign word in everybody's vocabulary, Kathy. Now let's see how well I've succeeded with Dane."

"I think she did a great job of it," Kathy said softly. "You don't know how to hate, either, do you?"

Earlier in the evening, after he had shaved and rested and checked with the hospital several times, Dane had built a roaring blaze in the fireplace. They had all felt its penetrating glow, sitting around the living room, talking, putting the misplaced pieces of their lives back in order. It was as if an unset mosaic pattern had been scattered. And now, bit by bit, they were replacing each tiny piece where it belonged, setting the colors and shapes into a harmonious design once more. And cementing them into place — hard and fast.

Petey had expressed his amazement with interspersed comments: *"Man!"* Or, "I still don't get it." But he "got it." It became clearly understandable when he tried to explain driving a stranger's car to Chatsville with a girl he had never seen before, when some of his best friends needed transportation to the hospital!

At ten o'clock, Mom got up from her overstuffed chair, signaling Petey to make an equally "discreet disappearance." They said good night, but not until Pete had asked, "Hey . . . let's settle one thing. If people ask me . . . you know, how come Kathy's a nurse, and why did she. . . ."

"You tell them the truth," Dane said firmly. "You tell them the way it *was*."

"That'll be good enough for our friends," Pete acknowledged.

Dane set his pipe down in a tray. "It was good enough for us, wasn't it?"

And the now-silent fire had burned itself

down to a single log, which glowed red under its heavy coat of gray ash. Dane waited until complete quiet had descended over the house. Upstairs, Petey had slammed his last door for the night, had dropped his last shoe.

Unexpectedly, Dane said, "We're going to be on a tight schedule at the hospital for a while. If I could get Larry Forbes to straighten out our situation — get your recommendation from Knollside — would you want to take a three-to-eleven shift for a while?"

"Just like that?" Kathy asked. "I'm hired? No questions asked?"

"We've all had our fill of questions. And problems. They aren't over, but, as Larry says, that's why attorneys are born. If I give him the medical reasons for what happened, he should be able to untie the legal tangles. The sooner the better. We need you at the hospital, Kathy." Dane rose and crossed the room, seating himself beside Kathy on the couch. "We have a heavy patient load, and the late shifts are short handed. I think we can get . . . what's her name . . . to move over to eleven to seven. What *is* her name . . . the girl Mrs. Borowski brought over one afternoon?"

"Claire Ballenger?"

Dane nodded, skipping over the name as though it held no meaning for him. "That's the one. And if we can get you on the second shift. . . ."

"I'll take any hours, Dane. Gratefully. Just to be in uniform again . . . and needed."

"You're needed here, too," Dane said. "At home. At the hospital. Helping me make it the kind of hospital I want it to be. The kind of hospital that can do even better than we did last night. One that has the right equipment and the right people — and that can be ready for an emergency. I need you to help me there, darling."

Dane's arm dropped over Kathy's shoulders. "Most of all, though . . . you're needed *here*." He drew her closer to him, kissing her gently the first time — and less gently the second.

After that, it was impossible for Kathy to be analytical. It was enough to be near Dane and to know that two other people who had loved each other would have wanted this for her.

For no one, she was certain, would have been as happy for Kathy at this moment as "Jim's girl."